Father Steve's Dilemma

Books by Jacqueline DeGroot

Climax
The Secret of the Kindred Spirit
What Dreams Are Made Of
Barefoot Beaches
For the Love of Amanda
Shipwrecked at Sunset
Worth Any Price
Tales of the Silver Coast, A Secret History of
Brunswick County with Miller Pope

The Widows of Sea Trail-Book One
Catalina of Live Oaks
The Widows of Sea Trail-Book Two
Tessa of Crooked Gulley

Running into Temptation with Peggy Grich
Running up the Score with Peggy Grich

To contact the author or read about her other books,
please visit *www.jacquelinedegroot.com*

Father Steve's Dilemma

by
Jacqueline DeGroot

©2009 by Jacqueline DeGroot

Published by American Imaging
Cover design: Jim Grich
Format and packaging: Peggy Grich

Printed in the United States of America

ISBN: 978-1-61539-772-3

This book is a work of fiction. All characters in this book have no existence outside the imagination of the author and have no relation whatsoever to anyone bearing the same name or names except where permission has been granted.

When the right woman comes along, she can change all manner of things, including a man's career. If he's a Catholic priest, he'd better have a back up plan. Please enjoy my spicy romance about a priest who prays for deliverance from his past, only to have God provide an entirely different dilemma. God and his sense of humor!

Thank you to my proofreaders:

Pat Callahan
Arlene Cook
Ray Cullis
Bill DeGroot
Debbie Echard
Jack Echard
Peggy Grich
Sue Kuebler
Diane Stander

and to Miller Pope for his rendition of
Father Steve for the cover.

Father Steve's Dilemma
by
Jacqueline DeGroot

Prologue

"Bless me Father, for I have sinned . . ." With those words Father Steve's life fell apart—all over again.

Chapter One

It had been a grueling day and Father Steve would have given anything not to have been the priest hearing confessions this evening at St. Paul's. Now, close to midnight, as he lay in his bed staring at the shadowed ceiling, his mind flashed back to earlier in the day when he hadn't known what he knew now, when he had been on the basketball court feeling the acrid sting of sweat as it ran into his eye, when he'd just been a teacher playing roundball with his students on a weedy patch of asphalt in the gritty inner city of Philadelphia.

Father Steve swiped at the sweat with the back of his hand, maneuvered himself and the ball to the side of the basket, turned quickly and jumped between the bodies, shooting the ball in a high arc. It careened off the backboard and went in amid whoops and hollers.

"That's the game fellas," he said, and wiped more sweat from his brow.

"Awww! One more, Father Steve. One more. Pleeease." The imploring face was covered with as much sweat and grime as his, only this one was black and young—probably all of fifteen.

"I don't think so, Shorty. Got to get cleaned up for this evening's confessions, you know."

"Please, Father Steve?" came the voice of another player.

Father Steve turned to the pixie-faced imp everyone called Micky. There was something about Micky; he could never refuse him. Maybe it was his earnest smile or laughing bright green eyes. Something about Micky pulled at him, made him wink just to coax his gamine grin. It was hard to believe that Micky was a sophomore in college, he had a youthfulness in his features that reminded Father Steve of a Copperfield waif, but his mind was quick, his wit sharp, and the energy he displayed on the court boundless.

"Okay. One more," he relented, "and this time I'm not giving up any points—you guys are getting way too good."

Twenty minutes into the game, out of the corner of his eye, he saw André trip and start to crash into Micky. André was nearly six feet tall; Micky almost five—the force of the sudden impact was sure to send Micky reeling. Father Steve dropped the ball and lunged to his left, grabbing Micky to keep him from falling to the hard, cracked asphalt.

With one hand he lifted Micky off his feet, and with the other he protectively clasped Micky's back against his chest. Then the oddest sensation shot through his arm as he realized the flesh he was grasping was a feminine breast—small, but nicely rounded and full. As the instant jolt of the encounter flashed through his body, he quickly released his cupped hand from *her*. Removing his other hand from around her waist, he stepped back and stared at her as she slowly turned to face him.

Their eyes met—his questioning, hers glaring. Then he watched as her defiant face turned into an imploring one, and he knew that Micky didn't want the others to know what he had just discovered.

"Hey, C'mon," Tyrone called out, "What's the holdup here? André, you gotta watch those big feet of yours. You almost knocked Micky down! Nice save, Father Steve."

André threw the ball back to Father Steve, and as he unconsciously caught it, he gave Micky a questioning look then tilted his head and raised a finely sculptured brow.

The game resumed and even though Father Steve's body was back in it, his head was not. Several times when his eyes met Micky's, he saw a scared and worried look. Dear God, what a shocking revelation!

He concentrated harder, played with abandon, and soon the game ended with his team the victors, again. As everyone disbanded to find the next distraction that would eat up the time on this late Friday afternoon, Father Steve called to Micky who was quickly making her way through a gaping hole in the wire mesh fence.

"Hey, Micky! Wait up!" he called.

"I can't. I gotta go," Micky called back.

"I'll walk with you," he called out and grabbed his sweatshirt from an old wooden bench. He jogged over to where Micky was trying to make her escape. Father Steve ducked through the hole in the fence, jogged a few paces and pulled up alongside her.

"So, what's this charade all about?" he asked.

"What are you talking about?"

"You know darned well what I'm talking about.

Why are you pretending to be one of the guys?"

"I'm not," she said.

"Oh yeah, you could've fooled me. In fact, you did, until today."

She looked at him with resignation in her eyes, and he could tell by the way her body suddenly slumped that she was admitting defeat. "You're not going to tell are you?"

He looked at her, a frown creasing his brow. "That depends. Why don't you want anyone to know you're a girl?"

"It's safer to be a guy."

"Well, I can't argue with you there, but why is it necessary? Do you feel threatened?"

"Not anymore."

"Who threatened you?"

"Nobody here. Not since I moved out of the dorm last year."

He knew that Micky was a student at St. Paul University. In fact, she was one of his students—one of his better students. "Elaborate for me if you would please, *Miss* Roberts. By the way, I never looked at your student profile. Is your name really Micky?"

"It's Michelle. My nickname used to be Missy. Last year I was Missy Roberts, and I almost got raped in my dorm room—more than once."

"Did you tell anybody?"

"No. It wouldn't have done any good, and it just would've made more trouble for me."

"So, for your sophomore year, you decided to become Micky. Micky the guy."

"Hey, don't knock it! Being one of the guys not only keeps me safe, it gives me a whole new view of the world."

Father Steve reached down and fingered Micky's cropped blonde hair. "So, you cut your hair," he stepped back and surveyed her, "bound your breasts in a tight-fitting sports bra and stopped shaving your legs and underarms."

"Oh, that's not all."

"Oh?"

"I've learned to belch, spit and cuss with the best of 'em."

He laughed with a deep throaty chuckle.

"Which restrooms do you use?"

"The men's, but I always use a stall."

"So you feel safer with your pants down in the men's room than you do in a coed dorm?"

"It's a small price to pay to be left alone."

"So where do you live now?"

"On campus."

He sensed that something was not right, her answer was too vague.

"Where?"

"The Hill."

"Where at The Hill?"

"The fifth floor."

"There is no fifth floor at The Hill."

"The second one then."

"Micky, where do you really live?"

She hesitated before blurting out, "All right, in my car."

"I thought as much."

"Why?"

"I don't know, you just seem down on your luck. That, and the fact that I got a slip in my box that said I needed to send you to the finance office the next time you came to class."

"They must be looking for my tuition payment."

"Do you have it?"

"No, not all of it. Not yet anyway."

"Do you have a job?"

"Sort of."

"What do you mean by that?"

"The Admin Office has jobs for me every now and then, and I do some yard work for one of the science professors."

"Well, that certainly can't add up to much."

"Things'll get better, they always do."

"Where's your family?"

"I wish I could say I knew, but I don't. As soon as I turned eighteen, my dad and step mom sold the house and bought an RV. That was two years ago. I've had two postcards since, one from Scottsdale and one from Hoover Dam. But I've basically been on my own since my dad remarried; my step mom and I don't get along very well."

"Where's your mom?"

"Oh, she died. Took too many pills, I think."

"Wow. You've had a rough time of it, haven't you kiddo?"

"Not any rougher than a lot of other people I suppose. It's not too bad. Two more years and I'll have my certificate and then I can teach. I can buy a house and groceries and a big ol' black German shepherd."

"So you can be Missy again?" he asked with a wry smile.

She smiled back at him and nodded, and the beauty of it momentarily stunned him.

He looked at her closely then, seeing her for what she really was, a young woman. A little sprucing up, a feminine haircut and just a bit of makeup and she'd be a petite knockout. She was slight of build and even though she couldn't be more than five feet, it seemed she was all arms and legs in her basketball shorts and jersey. She probably had some nice hips under all that loose clothing, but he was sure she dressed so it wouldn't show.

"Well, we'll have to work on getting you a sex change operation."

"What?"

"Getting you changed back into a girl."

"I like the way things are for now."

"They can't stay that way, you know."

"I know. I want to make sure they put the right name on my certificate. And when the chancellor shakes my hand, I want a picture that I can show my dad whenever he surfaces."

The sad twinge he heard in her voice made him look hard at her. How could anybody abandon this sweet kid? And what was worse, how was it that the approval of her father was still so important to her after he had deserted her? As far as he was concerned her father didn't deserve any consideration, and certainly he didn't deserve the wistful tone she had in her voice. But he saw the same thing over and over again when he counseled dysfunctional families. Family was family and no matter how bad they were—they were yours, and the desire to be accepted by your parents was universal—no matter how much they didn't warrant a child's adoration.

"Are you any good at making beds, scrubbing floors and the like?" he asked.

"Could be. I can learn to do just about anything. Why?"

"We're looking for someone at the rectory.

Someone who can do some cleaning, the laundry, and occasionally cook when the parishioners' casseroles give out."

"I could do that."

"Come by tomorrow afternoon and see the Monseigneur. I'll give him the low down."

"Thanks!"

"You're welcome. Hope it works out," he said as he turned to go in the opposite direction.

"Father Steve?"

"Yes?"

"Do I show up as Micky or Missy?" she asked with chagrin, a crooked smile brightening her face.

"Do you want a place to sleep also?"

"That would be nice."

"Then you might want to be Micky for a little while longer. He smiled at her and winked, "I'll keep your secret as long as I don't have to lie."

"Thanks. I wish I didn't have to either. But it's not really lying, if nobody asks."

"No, it's not. It's deception though, and that's not good."

"Maybe I'll see you in confession one day."

"Gosh, I almost forgot!" He glanced at his watch. Thirty minutes 'til confession, and he still had to shower and shave. He turned toward the rectory and began jogging. He was cursed with a five o'clock shadow that made its presence known around two in the afternoon, necessitating two shaving regimens on most days— certainly on Sundays when most men were able to take a day off from it entirely.

The young priest bounded up the red brick steps and ran through the arbored walkway to the rectory adjoining the cathedral. He didn't notice the man sitting on the wrought iron bench in front of the impressive front doors to St. Paul's old gothic cathedral. The grizzled man sat shrouded in the shadows of the late afternoon sun as it fought to penetrate the leafy canopies of the stately oaks lining the walkway. He looked up when he heard the echoing staccato of someone running and watched as a young man hurriedly opened the door and entered the rectory. The homeless man's thoughts were on St. Paul's and when he'd been a youth there so many years ago.

I rang the bells and I never missed, not even once. I was there every time they called, all my times and all their times, too. All the times they couldn't drag themselves out of bed because of the whorin' they did the night before. What hypocrites! They were the elite—the altar boys of St. Paul's. They were supposed to be so pure, so pious. But they weren't—they were just like all the others. Nasty and naughty while they fooled their parents and even the priests. But they never fooled me. I knew. I knew exactly what they were doing. I knew because I used to watch them. I used to watch them take those girls with their short, blue pleated plaid skirts and their tall gray knee socks tucked into black and white saddle oxfords with their starched white collared shirts—I used to watch them as they took them into the back seats of their cars and kissed them and stroked them until the girls let them take off their shirts and even their pointy-tipped bras. Yeah, I watched them as they scooted skirts up those smooth, bare thighs. I even watched them as those bad Catholic girls let those altar boys into their bodies, their

virgin crevices yielding to those rutting, arrogant pricks. They were being fucked and I saw it all. But I knew that one day I would get my reward. I would have a virgin, not some slimy slut. But a virgin. One saved just for me. Like Mary was saved for Jesus. Joseph was her first, but he didn't get to have her tight. My virgin will be tight. Tight, tight, tight. And she will exalt in me.

The man stood and shuffled into the church.

As Father Steve ran through the double doors leading to the rectory, he waved to one of the parishioners pruning the hedges that lined the brick walkway. "Hello Mrs. Reynolds," he called out. "Nice of you to lend us your green thumb this afternoon."

"Hi Father Steve. The Lord told me these hedges needed some trimmin', so here I am."

She watched him as he ran up the steps and disappeared into the rectory. *He also told me that you've got the best physique on a man that I have ever seen. What a waste of male virility,* she thought as she went back to her clipping. A widow in her forties, she was always trying to work her way into Father Steve's good graces. Surely, one day he'd topple off his ever-so-righteous white horse and need the companionship she was constantly hinting at, covertly of course, since neither one would want the censure of the church.

To her way of thinking, he was just about everything the male specimen should be. Tall, well built, Sicilian in ancestry from his mother's side, which gave him his natural dark coloring and thick black hair. English on his father's side, provided his light piercing eyes and graceful mannerisms. And smart—hell, half the time his students didn't know whether to call him Father or Doctor. He had a doctorate in Theology and a masters in European History, which is what he taught at St. Paul's Catholic University just a few short blocks away.

She knew a lot about Father Steve. She knew that he couldn't sit still; that he was always doing something. When he wasn't serving mass, teaching, instructing the altar boys, giving marriage classes, counseling, hearing confessions, performing marriages, presiding over funerals or visiting the sick, he was playing ball with the city's kids or running around the immense church parking lot. It seemed he was always attending to the parishioner's needs, all of them—except hers.

Her needs never seemed to coincide with his, and lately she found herself wondering if perhaps he might be gay. She had heard that many Jesuits were that way; who knew what happened during four years at the seminary?

There'd been many a time that she'd dolled herself up and paraded herself in front of Father Steve with the lowest décolletage that Christian propriety would allow. But all he'd ever said was, "You must be cold, you have goose bumps on your arms." Did it ever occur to him that her goose flesh was solely because of his nearness? Oh, no. He was way too pious. Either that, or immune to her charms—which she was loathe to believe—lots of men wanted her. Sure, she was slightly more than ten years older, but she was still a fine looking woman, and she knew it.

One hot summer night, when she and Father Steve had been seated across from each other at a pot luck dinner, she had purposely dropped her napkin under the table. When he chivalrously ducked under the table to retrieve it for her, she had met him under the table and given him an eyeful by casually letting one of her spaghetti straps fall off her shoulder, completely baring one voluptuous breast. But did he respond the way any able-bodied, full-blooded male should have? No, he didn't. He had simply taken his fingers and pulled the strap up for her. He hadn't even let his fingers linger on her shoulder. . . not even for a second. The next thing she knew, he went to the podium where he started calling out the numbers for bingo. One day— one carefully contrived day—she'd catch him in a weak moment. And it would be worth it, of that she was sure. A man just couldn't look that good and not know his way around a woman's body.

Father Steve shaved standing in front of the bathroom mirror with a towel draped around his waist. As he dipped the soapy blade into the basin, he thought about Micky and that one touch that had branded itself into his skin. He dropped the razor into the sink and looked at the palm that had grasped her breast. He could still feel its shape and visualize exactly where her nipple had pressed into it. He had to fight to control the sexual urges that welled inside him. Why was that little snippet causing him so much anguish? Determined to put her out of his mind, he reached for his aftershave lotion. The painful burn of the scented alcohol as it came into contact with his freshly abraded skin erased her from his mind, for the moment.

He went into his bedroom and donned one of his black frocks, attached the Roman collar, and slid his bare feet into soft, leather cordovan loafers. He always got grief from the Monseigneur whenever the benevolent old man looked down and spied Father Steve without any socks. But the old pater did listen to his reasoning when Steven insisted that no one would ever see his feet from the confessionals. Father Steve smiled when he thought about how shocked the old cleric would be if he ever found out that his young, fledgling ecclesiastic rarely bothered to wear any underwear under his frock either. It was just too darned hot under there. He went down to the kitchen to grab a quick glass of orange juice before heading over to the church.

On his way through the cool, darkened hallways, he thought back to the first event of the day that had unsettled him and left him feeling melancholy. It had been the catalyst that made him seek out the strenuous exercise of a late afternoon pick-up basketball game to release some tension.

Returning from teaching a morning class about the Renaissance, he'd found a letter on his desk in his combination bedroom-study. On close inspection, he found that it had been forwarded several times until it had finally reached him here, in care of St. Paul's Catholic Church. It was addressed to his deceased mother. He remembered the shiver that had gone through him as he'd read her name.

Using a letter opener, he had torn the top open and extracted a single-folded sheet of paper. Typed in the center, under the letterhead of a bank in Philadelphia, were these words: "Dear Mrs. Tyndale: Your ten-year Certificate of Deposit has matured. Please advise us as to whether we should reinvest it in another certificate program or hold it out for distribution." A Mrs. Shirley

Jacobsen, the bank manager, had signed it.

When he had called the number printed on the letterhead and spoke with Mrs. Jacobsen, he was informed that his mother had opened the account in both her name and his father's two years before she died. The application form noted that the money and its subsequent earnings were to be designated as a tax deferred annuity. At maturity, three months ago, it had a value of $266,873.86. As the only heir to their estate, it was his money now.

His and the church's if he chose it to be. His and the church's if he continued his vow of poverty. He had put the letter back into its envelope and tucked it into the top drawer of his desk, then changed into sweats, grabbed his sneakers, and ran at a breakneck pace all the way to the basketball courts several blocks away.

It was just too much to deal with right now, a quandary he didn't want to have to think about. He did wonder how his mother had managed to come up with so much money to invest just months before Kelly's lavish wedding though. His father had been a prominent dentist, but his parents had never acted as if they'd had money to spare. But they must have. They'd had a fine house, bought new cars every few years, and always kept their children in parochial schools. And, as far as he knew, they had never failed to pay the tuition payments on time, even when he had gone on to college. Yes, now that he really thought about it, there'd always been money, at least until that fateful day. After that horrible day, his father had never worked again.

Six hours after having read the unsettling letter, he opened a connecting door, walked into the solemn, incense-tinged church with its eighty-foot high beamed ceilings and imposing stained glass panels depicting the stations of the cross, and stopped to genuflect in front of the altar. He walked alongside the empty, heavy oak pews to a side aisle and ensconced himself into the center of three intricately carved confessional boxes.

After a few quick prayers, he slid open the screen and whispered, "Yes, my child?"

He was greeted by a gravely voice that pronounced the standard response, "Bless me Father, for I have sinned. It has been six weeks since my last confession. I have missed one holy day of obligation, I have had cross words with my husband, and I had an evil wish for my mother-in-law. I have lied about something and because of that lie, I have had to lie several other times." And so it continued for an hour. He listened, he commiserated, and he doled out penance. There was a lull for a few minutes and he wasn't sure if it was time for hearing confessions to be over with; he had forgotten to replace his watch after his shower. He could start to feel his legs stiffening and was wondering just how much longer he'd have to remain seated in this dark, closet-like box, when he heard someone open the door to one of the boxes beside his. He heard someone settle into the seat in front of the closed screen. He slid his screen open, permitting a vague outline of a man. He could hear raspy, deep breathing and smelled the strong odor of whiskey and tobacco. He turned his head and drew in a deep breath before moving closer and facing the screen. "Yes, my child?" he asked.

"Bless me Father, for I have sinned . . . It's been

eight years since my last confession and there's not much that I've done right since then. I have just started coming back to m' faith, and I wanted to make a clean breast of everything. First off, I'm an alki, and I've done some coke now and then, but the things I reckon me 'n God've got to talk about are my molesting . . . and once, I committed murder."

"I see," Father Steve was shaken, but kept his composure. "Are those things in the past, you're not doing them anymore?"

"I drink some now and agin, but I try not to let it get away from me. I don't do no drugs no more, and it's been four years since I messed with a kid. The murders were eight years ago."

"Murders?" Steve asked, accentuating the pluralness of the word.

"Yeah. A mother and her daughter. Her mother caught me with the girl and I panicked. I killed 'em both."

Steve's heart froze in his chest. He didn't even know how he managed to get the next words out, "Where did this happen?"

"A little house over on Lorisdale."

Steve never heard the rest of the man's diatribe about how sorry he was and how scared he'd been when the drugs had worn off. How he'd packed up all his things and moved to Oregon to live with his sister. How he'd been terrified the whole time he'd lived there, expecting each knock on the door to be the sheriff.

Steve heard the man, but his mind only absorbed the words then slowly discarded them all as only one thought prevailed and stayed, screaming into his numbed mind. *This was the man who had murdered his mother, and Kelly, his sister.* This was the man who was raping Kelly when his mother walked in on him in the basement of their house on Lorisdale Lane. This was the man who had bashed both their skulls in with a monkey wrench. This was the man who had driven his father insane.

Steven had been the one to find them when he came home from his college classes late that afternoon. There was blood everywhere and Kelly, twitching on the floor, had still been alive—unconscious, but alive. She died the next day in the arms of her fiancé without ever having regained consciousness. There was evidence of the rape but a negligible amount of semen, which led the investigators to believe that the rapist had been interrupted before or during ejaculating.

Four long years later, they finally shelved the case; there just weren't any clues. The wrench from his father's workbench was missing, and there were no fingerprints. The footprints they found in the back yard where a man had hopped the fence had been no help. They were too nonspecific. Buy-em-at-any-dime store work boots, they could have been anybody's. There might be something they could find today, with all the new technology, if the crime scene had been left intact—but it wasn't. As soon as everything had been cleaned and painted, his father had listed the house. It finally sold two years later at a substantially reduced price.

His father never recovered. Each day he grew worse. He told Steve at least a hundred times that if it weren't for his faith, he would have committed suicide; but he didn't think anybody would pray for his soul, so he knew he couldn't. When the case was closed, he had crawled into a tight shell and refused to talk to anybody. Instead, he just gave up and drank himself numb both day and night. He ended up in a nursing home thirty years too soon, broken and psychotic, before finally succeeding in taking his own life via the alcohol. He couldn't do it directly. Oh, no, that would have been an unforgivable sin.

And here, in front of him, was the man who had caused all this to happen. The man who had taken away his whole family and started a chain of events that had forever altered his own life and the plans he'd had for his future.

He'd had plans to get a doctorate in European History, find a small university, get a professorship, earn tenure, fall in love, take a wife, and raise a family. Instead he was forced to switch his doctorate to Theology, enroll in a seminary and become a priest. All because his father had managed to convince him that he needed to pray for his mother's and sister's souls, and that the prayers needed to come from a loftier source, someone closer to God. And because Steve needed to find a way to get some peace, he had reluctantly agreed and accepted his new role. He agreed to be their intercessor, to pray and to instruct others to pray on their behalf, to move their souls from the jaws of purgatory into the gates of heaven.

Behind the screen was the man who had altered the course of his life.

"Father? Did ya hear me? I said I plan on gettin' real active with the church again. I've prayed hundreds of Hail Marys and dozens of rosaries, but I know the penance is up to you to decide."

Penance? He was supposed to give this man penance, when every fiber in his body was screaming for him to reach through the screen and rip his throat out? An eye for an eye! That was scriptural. The words,

"Turn the other cheek," came to him also. Turn the other cheek? No! No! No way!

He didn't know what to do. He had to think. He had to reason this out. God, what was he supposed to do?

"My penance, father?"

"Yes. I'm thinking. Your sins require a moment of thought." What if this man had truly repented? As a priest, he was honor-bound to forgive him. As a man, he simply could not. After several moments, he said, "Your penance will be more than just prayer."

"I know. Now, I don't have much money, but I got skills. I can build things."

"Yes, yes that's good. We can use a man like that around here. There's always something that needs to be done. Are you in counseling now?"

My God, did he really want this man hanging around his church family? He thought of all the children in the parish—all the Catechism classes he taught on Saturday mornings, all the children who attended mass every morning before running across the street to the parochial school at St. Paul's. Yet, he didn't want this man to simply disappear, never to be found again, not without knowing who he was. He wanted him arrested. He wanted him in jail. No—he wanted him to die!

"I was in counseling until just recently. My sister passed, and I've just moved back into the area."

"Well, there's a lot of work you can do around here. Call the church secretary and tell her you want to help out and get back in counseling. I'll leave a number with her for you. Ask her for Father Bryant's number over at St. Matthew's, he does counseling for child molesting. And say one Act of Contrition daily as well as a rosary for each of the souls you took for as long as you live."

"Am I forgiven, Father?"

"God forgives you." *But I don't.*

When the man left the confessional, Father Steve quietly opened the door and left the confines of the priest's enclosure. He watched the gaunt, grizzled man from behind a large round pillar. He didn't think he'd ever seen him before, but it was hard to tell without seeing his face. As the man turned he saw his profile, and he knew he'd never forget that face. The face of the man who had taken a virgin against her will just days before her wedding and then slaughtered two innocent women to hide his crime. No, he'd never forget the face of the man who had raped his sister and murdered both her and his mother.

Sitting at his desk late that night, he tapped a pencil against his lips as he thought things over. Then his blood began to boil. He shot up out of his chair, shoving it back so hard that he had to grab it just before it fell to the floor. One-handed he slammed it down hard enough that he heard the wood crack. Shoving long fingers through his thick hair, he began to furiously pace. Sweat began to bead on his brow while his thoughts overwhelmed him. He was wrestling with the images of his mother and his sister sprawled in puddles of blood on the basement floor. How was he supposed to deal with this?

He thought this time that God had given him more than he could handle. His vows dictated that he forgive and accept this man back into the fold, but there was no way he could do that. No way!

Right now, it was everything he could do just to keep his hand from picking up the phone and turning him in. This was the man they had looked for for so long. This man deserved to be punished! And he didn't want to wait until it was time for him to sit before the throne and be judged. He wanted him judged now! Judged, found guilty, and executed. He was slime. As far as he was concerned, the man was not one of God's children; he was the spawn of the Devil!

Years ago, he had been told that the strongest expletive in the Bible was, "The Devil take you." They were certainly not the strongest words coming to his mind right this very minute.

Words of scripture reeled at him—words of compassion, words of forgiveness, words of deliverance. Things he had been taught over and over again, that had been drilled into him ad nauseam. Just who was he in the grand scheme of things? Who was he to determine this man's fate?

He couldn't disclose a confession, no matter what was confessed. It was more than just his job, it was a solemn oath—a promise that he had made.

But he couldn't keep this to himself either. He ran his hand through his hair, tugged it hard with frustration, and gave a great, exhausted sigh. Could he go to someone higher up? The Monseigneur perhaps? No . . . his vows precluded that, he couldn't go to anybody. Well, not anybody mortal anyway. He jumped up and grabbed his robe. It was after midnight, and he knew no one else would be up. God wouldn't mind if he came to talk to him with his pajamas on. He went down to the church and sat in his favorite chapel, the one that faced the statue of the Virgin Mary surrounded by hundreds of now unlit offertory votives.

For hours he knelt, deep in prayer and lost in thought. How long he stayed there, he could not say, but he knew that nothing had been resolved when he finally stood up. His knees ached, and he was still confused, agitated beyond belief and uncertain what his next move should be. But one thing he did know. He knew that as much as he enjoyed the children and the parishioners, and as dedicated as he was to his faith and performing his duties, he was no longer cut out to be a priest. He just didn't have it in his heart to forgive such a grievous sin. Not that it was his job to do the forgiving—that was God's. But what if he couldn't intercede for this man? What if he couldn't stand the thought that one day all would be forgiven as if nothing had ever happened?

And now, now as he lay in his bed during the darkest part of the night, staring at the ceiling, he felt more alone and more confused than he'd ever been in his life. A fitful rest followed, interrupted a few hours later by the buzzing of his bedside alarm.

Chapter Two

Father Steve came back to his room after a late morning jog to find the door open and someone bending over his bed, stripping it. He was about to ask what they were doing when the person turned to face him and he saw that it was Micky.

"Father Steve," she said breathlessly, "I got the job."

"So I see," he said with a grin. Now that he took the time to actually look her in the face, he wondered how he had ever thought she was anything other than a woman. Her features were soft, especially her lips and no man would know what to do with lashes so thick and so long. He wondered how it was that he hadn't noticed them before.

"Monseigneur was so nice. He thinks very highly of you. Apparently all I needed was your recommendation."

"Well, we're all getting a little tired of running the vacuum in our so-called 'spare time' and all the dust is beginning to make us think we've got a lot of dead people living here with us."

"Pardon?"

"Ashes to ashes . . . dust to dust."

"Oh, yeah. Right." She smiled, and he felt the goodness of her seep into him. She was a breath of fresh air in this stale, stodgy place.

"Any problems with the accommodations?"

"No, none at all. He gave me my own room back behind the kitchen area. It even has its own bathroom. This is livin' high on the hog for me."

He gave her a big grin and moved to the other side of the bed to help her make it with fresh linens.

"You don't have to do that. This is my job."

"Well, I figure the sooner we get this bed made, the sooner I can shoo you out of here so I can strip and take a shower. Others may not be so thoughtful, since they won't think anything of another male being in their room." But oddly enough, the thought of being naked in front of her wasn't a distressing thought. In fact, the part of him that made him male was relishing the idea.

"Good point. I'd better be careful about that. Especially around Father Justy."

They both had a good laugh over that. Neither had a desire to see the rather obese, roly-poly and jocular Jesuit in the all-together.

Later that day, Father Steve performed a high mass for a parishioner's daughter's wedding. The church was elaborately decorated with white calla lilies and silver ribbons. The tall, ornate candelabras had been pulled out of storage and polished to a bright sheen, and there were six different groupings of musicians all designated to play a special song to honor the bride and groom. He couldn't help but feel that this was the type of wedding his sister had missed. It had all the touches of a doting mother whose mission was to send her daughter off properly, in elegant style.

As the altar boys handed him the covered chalice

and knelt to the tinkle of the silver bells, he prayed a quick silent prayer for the young couple kneeling in front of the altar. He knew them both; he'd counseled them for this marriage. He prayed that they have a happy union and that they never have to experience the hardships that his family had. He prayed that they would have lots of children who would all grow up to be good Catholics.

He turned to face the couple and administer the sacrament of the Holy Eucharist to them. The stark white of the woman's wedding gown shimmered in the sun as the late rays shone through the windows. He doubted that she was still a virgin and hence entitled to wear white, but still the thought of purity was there. She had just pledged herself wholly to her husband for now and forever, until the end of time. He wasn't foolish enough to believe that none of the marriages he performed ever ended in divorce, but every time he celebrated this union with a bridal couple, he thought of the times that he had envisioned himself standing just to the right of a beautiful bride, vowing to love, honor and cherish her until death. And not surprisingly, a few times he had to bite back the emotion of jealousy when the groom lifted the veil and kissed his new bride.

Back in the sacristy, the room used to change vestments, he joked with the four altar boys as they changed out of their robes, ribbing one for being late ringing the bells for a *kyrie eleison* and another for clicking his retainer against his teeth when the bride and groom kissed. "That kiss made you a little dry mouthed eh, Gary?" The altar boy blushed and sneered at his jeering compatriots.

An older man lingered in the doorway watching them, but they paid him no mind. The man was looking at the pile of discarded robes and surveying the room, remembering a time long past, a time when he'd been an altar boy and dedicated to God. *The same smells, beeswax wax and incense mingled with Brut 33, the same hallowed and reverent feeling in his gut,* the man thought as he hid around the corner listening to the camaraderie between the priest and his young charges. His mind drifted back thirty-five years and an image of himself filled his mind. He was in his long black robe with the white starched collar, freshly washed and liberally doused with cologne that sat on the shelf of the closet. He was hidden this time, too. He was in one of the stalls, his eye to the crease where the stall walls gaped as he watched young Bobby Reid jerk off with his father's *Playboy* propped open on the back of the toilet. Later, he had asked if he could borrow the magazine and was told to "Get your own porn, you pervert!" He hated Bobby Reid and the easy way he had with girls. Now he hated him for his sizeable cock and his ability to shoot his cum from the toilet to the wall behind it. He was rarely able to get his so hard, and never able to do more than dribble.

Chapter Three

After the reception, Father Steve went to the common room in the large rectory. He needed to catch up on the things going on around the church and in the city with his congregational family—the parish priests, the Monseigneur, the visitors from other churches, and the lay people who acted as staff and helped run the large church.

In every church there are members who are always there, who can always be called upon when there's work to be done. They are devoted and eager to share their time because they're lonely, or they feel it's their duty to help wherever they're needed. And then there were some misguided ones trying to "buy" their way into heaven, by sacrificing their time or money. This church had more of the truly devoted kind of parishioners than Father Steve had ever seen anywhere else. The women who took charge of the vestments and the church furnishings were some of the most dedicated people he knew. The men who volunteered their time in shifts to mow the lawns and paint were hardworking, God-fearing people who could be counted on for practically anything. But the women who cooked were his favorite. They could always be depended upon to make the comfort foods he remembered from his childhood.

As he walked into the large hall he immediately noticed that two things were different. One was the smell. There was a nice lemony tang reminiscent of furniture polish. He couldn't help but deeply inhale the clean, fresh scent. Even though there was always help on hand, the task of dusting and vacuuming on a regular basis was hard to foist on someone who had to go home and do it there too. The citrusy scent spoke of a thorough polishing job. The other thing that was different was that Mrs. Reynolds was there. Mrs. Reynolds with her overly applied makeup and fragrance.

This was such a busy, bustling church that there were always many functions going on and so many people coming and going from the priests' offices and the Monseigneur's office, that it wasn't at all unusual to have twenty or more people gathered in little groupings all over the large room. That was, until after eight o'clock. After eight o'clock, it became a home again, a more or less private home for those who lived in the rectory. Until then, you never knew whom you'd see, and no one would be thought to be out of place. Except in his mind, Mrs. Reynolds was always out of place. She was one of those people he couldn't quite figure out. She didn't seem like a true believer in any sense of the word. He didn't even know why she was here tonight, but he suspected it was as it always was, to flirt with him. There were these types of women in all parishes. The ones who thought it was a real turn on to try to turn on the priest. Some wouldn't have a clue what to do if a priest actually accepted their advances, but he felt certain that Rita Reynolds would know.

Out of the corner of his eye he spied movement, after a closer look, he smiled, seeing that it was Micky, sitting at the end of a long worktable, polishing the house silver. She was surrounded on her end of the table by candlesticks, candy dishes and a sterling silver tea set. She looked up and gave him a shy smile. He winked at her and made his way to his favorite chair in front of the fireplace to read the newspaper. Even though there was no fire, it was still his favorite chair and everybody respected that. It was always vacant and waiting for him whenever he got back from ministering to the congregation. After the wedding reception, he'd gone to two hospitals where parishioners were patients and then to visit one that was sick at home. At least two nights out of every week he was invited to someone's house for dinner, so time to relax in his chair and be somewhat alone with his reading was precious to him. Everybody knew this, even Rita Reynolds knew this. So why the heck was she here?

Turning the page of his newspaper, he looked over at Micky. She was looking at him with imploring eyes. He frowned and shot her a questioning look and then he saw what was bothering her. Mrs. Reynolds was flirting with Micky! She had her hand wrapped around Micky's as she tried to ostensibly show her how to properly polish the tall candlesticks. The caressing action was making Micky feel uncomfortable, and Father Steve had to bite his tongue to keep from laughing. He raised an eyebrow as if to ask, just what the heck are you two doing over there? But Micky obviously had no say in the stroking caresses running down her arm to her hand. She shrugged her shoulders and cringed, and Father Steve took pity on her.

"Micky," he called over to her.

"Yes?"

"Did you get a chance to go to the cleaners and pick up the dry cleaning today?"

"No, Father, I didn't. I'll go get it now, before they close."

"That would be great. I'm down to my last clean frock. A baby got sick on me after I christened it this morning, would you mind dropping it off for me?"

"No, not at all. Where is it?"

"I left it on top of the washing machine in the utility room."

She gently untangled her hand from Mrs. Reynolds', hopped up and quickly left the room. At the door she turned and mouthed *thank you* to him and then she was gone.

He smiled at the little imp. If Rita Reynolds only knew she'd been coming on to a girl!

Chapter Four

The following Friday night, the murderer came back to the confessional. Father Steve had finally been able to put some distance to his feelings, but now they came back full force.

"Bless me Father, for I have sinned."

He hesitated before answering. Did he really want to hear this? What had the man done this time? "Yes?"

"Father, I was here last week and I told you about m' sins. I know your name is Father Steve, I've seen you around this week, and I was just wonderin' if I could talk to you, kind of private like."

"What's troubling you?" he asked, clearly not happy to be talking to this man.

"I know what I did was real bad, so bad I keep feelin' that God hasn't forgiven me yet, even though I've asked him to."

"Are you truly sorry for what you've done? Because if you're not, he knows it and he will withhold his forgiveness."

"I am sorry. Well, I am sorry about most things, but I ain't sorry about one."

"What's that?"

"I ain't sorry that I took a virgin."

Father Steve swore under his breath as he thought about Kelly being "taken" by this man, Kelly having her treasured virginity stolen from her just days before she was to give it to her new husband as her gift to him on their wedding night. And he had to cough to cover the objectionable sounds he was inadvertently making. "I don't understand. You *raped* a woman, but now you're not sorry about that?"

"She was mine. She was given to me."

"I don't think so," he said tersely, ready to get up, drag the man outside and beat him to a pulp.

"You don't understand the way it was that day. She was the virgin God selected for me."

"You're right, I don't understand. Why don't you tell me more about that day, tell me how *God* selected your virgin." He hadn't known his sister was a virgin, but he hadn't had any reason to think otherwise, except for the fact that she and Frank had been engaged for almost two years.

"God had been promising me a virgin because I worked for him for years, and I was just waitin' for him to make good on his promise when everything just lined up."

"Everything just lined up?"

"Yeah. I was workin' for UPS delivery. I was in this bridal shop while this mother and daughter was selectin' the daughter's weddin' dress. They was laughing an' joking about should it be a white dress or not, when the daughter said, 'White of course! Momma, you know I'm a virgin, Frank wouldn't have it any other way.' Well, my name is Frank, so I knew she was mine. I follows them home, parks my delivery van over on the next block, and I walks through the back yards. I heard the momma tell the girl that she's gotta take a swatch from the bridesmaid's gowns to the florist to match it up with the ribbons and flowers, so I waited and watched her leave. Then I walked into the house and found my virgin in the basement foldin' some clothes. She fought me, but I finally took her. Then her momma came back, I didn't know how quick her errand was goin' t' be. I didn't have no choice, she wouldn't stop yellin' and hittin' on me."

There was absolute silence between them for several minutes then Father Steve said, "Your name is Frank? You raped an innocent girl because she was promised to a man named Frank?"

"She was promised to me!"

"No. She wasn't."

"She wasn't?"

"No. She wasn't."

"What am I going to do?"

"I think you need more help than I can give you. You need professional help."

"I don't have the kind of money for that."

"Then turn yourself in and get it."

"I can't do that."

"Why not?"

"They'll put me in jail. They might even kill me."

"Don't you think you deserve that?"

"Well, maybe I do, but I'm not brave enough to do that."

"Not even for God's forgiveness?"

Frank thought for a few minutes. "I'm not sure. Won't he forgive me anyway?"

"Maybe."

"But you can forgive me."

"No, I can't do that."

"Only God, right?"

"Only God."

There was a long silence then Father Steve said, "Frank?"

"Yeah?"

"You aren't really sorry are you?"

"No."

"You're going to do it again, aren't you?"

"I don't know. I was promised a virgin."

"Did you see Father Bryant?"

"Yes."

"Did you tell him everything?"

"No."

"Well, let's start there. Go back and see him and this time tell him everything."

"Okay."

"Frank, do it!" He saw the silhouette of the man in the box jump. The firmness in his voice surprised even him.

"Okay, I will. Can I come back and talk to you next week?"

There was silence again.

"I'd rather you talk to him."

"I like you better."

"I'm not able to deal with this for reasons you don't understand."

"Don't cut me off. I need to talk to you."

"Fine. Fine. Just go see Father Bryant."

"Okay. Father?"

"Yes?" he asked, exasperated.

"Did you see the bookshelves I built in the Monseigneur's study?"

"No, I didn't."

"Some of my finest work, if I say so myself."

Father Steve heard Frank get up, open the door and shuffle away. He released a long, drawn out sigh then he heard the sounds of someone else opening the door and seating themselves.

"Bless me Father, for I have sinned . . . "

Chapter Five

Half an hour later he left the confessional with his shoulders aching and his posture slumped. It was a good night for sinners, he thought, but a bad night for their confessor. He rubbed his neck as he made his way through the aisles and to the connecting door to go back to the rectory.

"Father?"

Startled, he jumped. "Who is it?" he called.

In a shadowed corner of a small nave, a small voice called out, "It's me, Micky."

"Micky? What's the matter?"

"Nothing. I was just praying, and then I looked up and saw you. You look awful, is something wrong?"

"Yeah," he said as he reached over and ruffled her hair, "and I don't know how to fix it." His fingers lingered in her short curls as he marveled at the silky softness of her hair.

"Maybe I can help. You helped me."

"I think only God can intervene on this one, but thanks anyway."

"Sure."

He sensed her withdrawal and wondered if he had somehow hurt her feelings. "Tell you what, maybe you can help with something else. A distraction would be very nice right about now. Do you play chess?"

"No, but I've always wanted to learn," she answered wistfully.

He groaned. "That's more of a distraction than I was bargaining for . . . " He looked at her and couldn't help but laugh at her sullen pout. "Okay, c'mon, I'll teach you. But you'd better be a fast learner, I still have a sermon to work on tonight."

They went to the common room and sat across from each other at a small table, and he showed her how to set up the board. Two hours later he was surprised at how fast the time had flown and at how much strategy she had zeroed in on. Given a few months of playing and she would be a very worthy opponent. He said it was time to call it a night, and she helped him put the chess set back in its box. He stood to place the box on the top shelf of the bookcase to the left of the fireplace and was reminded of the bookcases Frank had said he'd made for the Monseigneur. He made a mental note to make sure he checked them out sometime tomorrow.

As he turned back to her, he caught her in a full body stretch, her hands were up in the air, and her back arched out over the back of her chair. From his perspective standing above her, he was able to see her breasts lifting together. He couldn't help but look down her shirt and see the cleavage she was inadvertently displaying. Instantly, heat rose in his groin. He had to bite his lip to keep from groaning both at the pleasure the sight was causing him, and at his immense disappointment to his body's traitorous response. He did not know at the time that the sight of the swell of her small breasts straining against her shirt would replay over and over in his mind as he sat at his desk trying to concentrate on his sermon.

Chapter Six

Marvelous craftsmanship don't you think?" the Monseigneur asked as Father Steve ran his fingers over the dark wood.

I suppose everyone has redeeming qualities, Father Steve thought bitterly to himself, but to the Monseigneur who was obviously very pleased with his new bookcases, he said, "Yes, they're very nice. Do you have that book I asked you about at breakfast, the one on legal and moral protocol?"

"Yes, yes." The Monseigneur's fingers ran along the spines of several large books until they located the volume he was looking for. "Ah, here it is, the what-to-do-when-you-don't-know-what-to-do-book of priestly duties. Can't tell you how many times I had to take this to bed with me when I was younger. After eight years of seminary, it seemed to me I hadn't learned much of anything when they dropped me off here and told me this was now my church. Don't know how I would've make it without this book."

"You took over during the war, didn't you?"

"Yes, World War II. I don't think there's ever been a time since that people were more confused. With almost all the men overseas, every confession was a soap opera and every telegram was bad news. There was a wedding service or a funeral almost every day, and I know for a fact that many times I baptized babies with the wrong last name." He patted the front of the old book, "Yes, this book was my constant companion. Whenever I was supposed to tell someone how to handle something that I had no idea how to handle myself, I found the answers here. What kinds of things are *you* up against in your ministry, anything you can tell me about?" he asked in a curious tone.

"Oh, nothing specific," he hedged, "just doing some research for a friend."

"Ah well, here you are, just replace it when you're done with it."

Father Steve took the cherished book out of the old man's wrinkled hands and thanked him. Then he took the book outside to sit in the garden among the statues of the Apostles to read it. It was a beautiful spring day and he was surrounded by shrubs in full bud. It was the kind of day that he'd probably find half his students staring out of the classroom windows with a glazed look in their eyes. He had a few hours before his afternoon class and he was determined to find a solution to his problem, or barring that, at least a complete understanding of exactly what his problem was.

An hour later he gently closed the book and looked up at the clear blue sky. It was just as he'd thought. He couldn't tell a soul, not even the Monseigneur. He couldn't act or respond to any of the information in any way that might jeopardize the man who had confessed his evil sins to him. He couldn't warn anybody, he couldn't alert anybody, he couldn't cause any suspicion. All he could do was try to talk

Frank into coming clean on his own, and to advise him to get help for his problem. If Frank decided not to do either, there was nothing he could do about it. Unless he had irrefutable proof that someone else was in danger.

A bell rang and he watched as the children in the quad diagonally across from him ran out onto the playground behind the school. Hundreds of little boys and girls unaware of the menace in their community, and there wasn't a damned thing he could do about it. He sighed and shook his head, then lifted the book that had somehow become much heavier. He went back to the Monseigneur's office and replaced it.

He looked through the rest of the books to see if there was something else he could read that might help, but there wasn't anything specific to this type of case. As he turned to leave, he was startled to see a man leaning against the doorframe. There was something familiar about him, but he didn't readily recognize the man as he stood in the shadowy hallway. But when the man spoke he knew exactly who he was.

"Like the shelves? I'm particularly proud of the way the frames around the glass turned out." It was Frank. Father Steve appraised Frank as he walked to one of the shelves and pulled on the decorative knob. The glass front slid into place over the books on that shelf.

"The edges are beveled perfectly and look at this dovetailing detail," Frank said as he ran a dirty fingernail along the side of the frame.

Father Steve could not hide his revulsion. To meet this man face to face was not the same as talking to him through a shadowed screen. He felt his jaw clench, and he tried to keep the hardness out of his eyes, but he didn't think he succeeded.

"Not too bad, wouldn't you say?"

Father Steve mumbled, "Nice, very nice," then excused himself to walk around to the other side of the desk, scribbled a note of thanks to the Monseigneur, and hurried out of the room.

Chapter Seven

In his own room, at the window, he ran his fingers through his hair, and noticed that he was trembling. Actually *trembling*. He looked down on the courtyard below and swore using words he hadn't used in years, but he meant every one of them. He was just about to turn away from the window when he spotted Micky, her arms laden with books, hurrying across the lawn. She was going to class. His class. And if he didn't hurry, his students would be in a trance, staring out the windows long before he could begin to bore them with his lecture.

He grabbed his briefcase and dashed out the door, ran down the hallway and headed over to the campus. He walked into his classroom and dropped his briefcase on his desk and looked up to see everyone smiling at him.

The students were amused at his appearance. The professor had never been late before, and he certainly had never shown up with his hair spiked all around his head like that. He was always well groomed and devastatingly handsome—although his dishevelment did not keep him from being handsome. It lent a rakishness to his good looks that

Micky found intriguing.

He looked around the room at all the curious faces and when his eyes found Micky's, she frantically motioned with her hand, pretending to smooth her hair. He got the message, and with both hands smoothed back his hair, digging his fingers in up to the knuckles in the thick, errant waves, then he spoke.

"Florence in the sixteen hundreds . . . what was the social tone? What were the people worried about? Mr. Brownley, read what you have prepared for us."

He accidentally referred to Micky as Miss Roberts instead of Mr. Roberts once during the class, but quickly covered up by saying, "Excuse me, I was looking at the seating chart wrong, Miss *Cohen*, what important artist came out of this enlightened period?"

Seventy minutes later, the class was dismissed, and he sat staring at Micky. She looked back at him as she leaned against the wall behind a seat in the back row. "I enjoyed the class, you find ways to make it sound so interesting. Was it really that turbulent in Europe back then?"

"The people endured one revolution after another as they tried to establish equality. But they failed to achieve the freedoms they felt they deserved with each new regime."

"I'd love to go to Europe one day."

"Yes, I believe you would. There are signs everywhere of the historical things you're learning here. There are churches that have written records of the people's lives, homes still standing from the days when all this was happening. It's really quite fascinating."

"Have you ever been to Europe?"

"Yes, twice actually. Once, to do research for my doctorate and once with our church group. One day you must find a way to get there."

"I will." She smiled and turned to leave.

"Thanks for the heads up on my hair."

She laughed, "It was pretty bad!" As she made her way behind the tight confines of the last aisle that was lined haphazardly with one-armed desks, she spotted a cell phone on a seat. She picked it up and waved it at him. "Here, someone left this," she said, and placed it on the edge of the last desk in the row and left.

Father Steve walked over, picked it up and flipped it open to see if there was a name on it. There was none. He pushed the power button to turn it on figuring that whoever lost it would simply call their number to see if it had been found. He tucked it into his briefcase along with his books, zipped it up and left the room.

On his way back to the rectory, he realized he was hungry, and that what he was hungry for was pizza. And not just any pizza, but the kind they served by the slice at Corrado's in the mall. He dropped his briefcase off in his room, grabbed the keys to one of the rectory's cars, and started to drive over to the mall. Pulling out of the lot, he thought about the phone, and on impulse went back to get it. Slipping it into his pocket, he got back into the car and drove to the mall. In an isolated parking space on the fringes of the parking lot, he sat in the car and stared at the phone in his hand.

He knew the number to the crime solver's tip line by heart, almost everybody did, it was drilled into their subconsciousness over and over again by all the radio ads. What he didn't know is whether he should call or not. From everything he had read earlier, he would be breaking his vows if he repeated confidential information he had heard in the confessional. He would be altering the future if he disclosed anything he had learned behind that screen about the murders of his mother and sister. But how could he just let the man wander around free, possibly with the intention of repeating his past crimes?

He would not be serving the community if someone was raped when he could have prevented it. And just how would he deal with the guilt of that? Wouldn't it be worse than the guilt of going against his vows? He flipped open the phone and stared at the keys for a few moments, mentally punching in the numbers he knew would connect him to the tip line. He pressed the power button and shut it off. He flipped it closed, placed it in his lap and prayed. After a few minutes he picked it up, powered it up again, and rapidly punched in the numbers. With the phone to his ear, he waited for it to ring on the other end. He wasn't worried about the call being traced to him because it wasn't his phone, but still, he was mindful not to be on the line too long.

When someone answered, he succinctly said, "There is a man named Frank who does handy man work at St. Paul's Church. He raped and killed Kelly Tyndale and her mother eight years ago." He heard the voice on the other end asking questions, but he simply pressed the power button and flipped the phone closed. He went into the mall, found a security guard and handed him the phone saying, "Someone lost this." Then he went to stand in line for two pieces of pepperoni pizza. While he was waiting, he made a mental note to tell his class that the police department was in possession of a cell phone that had been left in his classroom that day.

He'd alerted the police but was surprised he

didn't feel better, yet he didn't feel any worse either. He tried to put it out of his mind while he ate his pizza. It didn't taste as good as it usually did, and he tossed most of it out before leaving to prepare for a funeral service.

Chapter Eight

By one in the morning he'd had enough tossing and turning and decided to go down to the kitchen for a glass of milk. He was antsy and didn't know what to do with his restlessness, even though he was pretty sure what had caused it. If it wasn't so late, he'd love to shoot a few hoops over at the playground, but he knew that the steady *thump, thump, thump* of the ball on the pavement would wake everyone. As he rounded the corner to the kitchen, he was surprised to see a faint glow of light coming from the room. Reaching the doorway, he looked inside and saw Micky sitting alone at the table sipping from a cup. She looked at him as he came into the room.

"Can't sleep either?"

"No. Must be the pizza I had for lunch."

"I don't believe that. I've seen what you eat; you have a cast iron stomach. You smelled my hot chocolate, and just had to come down and get some," she said with a welcoming smile.

"Maybe you're right. I'll try some, if it's all right."

"Sure." She stood up to fix him a cup. He couldn't help but notice her gown. It was many sizes too big and was pinned in the center where it dipped into a big vee. When she got closer to the stove where the overhead light was, the gown became diaphanous. It was so transparent that he could see the outline of her legs, her thighs, her belly and her breasts. He could even define the darker area at the juncture of her thighs where her pubic hair was. She was in stark profile now, and he knew that once she turned to face him, he'd be able to see the dark circles of her nipples as well as the fullness of her breasts. His breathing became harsh, and he had to stifle his gasp. His fingers gripped the edge of the counter hard enough to turn his knuckles white. He forced his eyes down to the floor and found himself staring at her bare feet, and God, even they were sensuous to him.

He quickly whipped off his own robe and placed it over her shoulders before he realized what he was doing. So there he was, bare-chested in front of her with just his pajama bottoms on. He saw her eyes bug wide and he looked down. Not only was his broad, furred chest drawing her attention, but so was his blatant erection, tenting the fabric of his pajama bottoms as his arousal threatened to poke out of the opening. The thin cotton was the only thing separating them.

"Oh, my," he said. "I'm sorry," he mumbled and quickly turned around. At the doorway, he said, "I'll be right back, don't give away my hot chocolate. Just let me go put some clothes on."

Micky stood with her mouth open, then she smiled and pulled his robe tightly around her. It was still warm from his body and smelled of him, a pungent musky smell that was all male mixed with something reminiscent of fresh cut balsam. She hugged the robe to her and looked down to where the robe parted. She gasped when she saw the dark shadowing several inches below her navel and realized that he had seen it, too. She opened the robe wide, let it drop to the floor and looked down at her chest and then below to her thighs and groaned. If he'd doubted her sex before, he certainly didn't anymore. She hastily bent to retrieve the robe and quickly put it back on.

They both blushed furiously when he returned dressed in trousers with a crew sweater and loafers. He avoided saying anything and after a while she couldn't stand the uncomfortable edge they had between them now, so she cleared the air. "After you left, I realized what you saw. I didn't realize the effect that backlighting would have on this flimsy gown. I apologize."

He gave her a lopsided grin, "I knew you weren't doing it on purpose. And I'm sorry I reacted the way I did."

"I'm flattered. Sometimes I miss being seen as a girl. It's nice to be reminded every once in a while that I still am one."

"Oh you are, most definitely."

"Here's your hot chocolate," she said as she handed him a steaming mug.

"Thank you." He took a small sip and nodded his head. "It's good, very good." From where he stood he could still see the big pin between her breasts. He nodded at it and said, "I gather that's not your gown. It looks way too big for you."

Sheepishly, she drew the robe tighter over her breasts. "It's not, I got it from the lost and found at the dorm last year. It's a size eighteen."

"What size do you wear?"

"A six."

"So it's three times the coverage you need."

"Apparently not."

They both looked at each other and laughed. They sipped their chocolate in silence looking over the rims of their mugs at each other. When the comfort level made him nervous again, he placed his cup on the counter and said good night. She walked down the hallway and watched him climb the steps. One thought kept coming back to her over and over again. *My body, my little girl's body made him hard!* It was such a heady feeling to know she had the power to turn on this magnificent man, this man who was supposed to be steeled against these types of feelings. And, even though she feared that she could be damned for her thoughts, she reveled in them.

Chapter Nine

Two days later, Father Steve received a phone call from a detective who had worked on his mother's and sister's case.

"Father Steve, this is Detective Samuels from the 5th, we got an anonymous tip that a man working at your church might know something about your family's murders, that he might even have had something to do with them. You got a man workin' there named Frank?"

"Yes," he said, realizing that his hand was already beginning to sweat as it gripped the handset.

"Well, here's the deal. I need to question him but I don't want to scare him off."

"I understand."

"So maybe you could ask him some questions for me."

That wasn't going to help! "What?" he asked, feigning confusion.

"Like maybe you can find out some things."

"Detective Samuels, have you forgotten that I'm a priest? I can't help you. I can't tell you anything that he tells me."

"Oh yeah, I kinda forgot about that."

"I read that now you have a way of checking a suspect's DNA against sperm samples, even negligible ones."

"Yeah, sometimes. But this isn't one of those sometimes."

"Why not?"

"We can't find the semen sample."

"What!"

"Well, it's here somewhere. I'm sure it will turn up, we just can't put our hands on it right now."

"Great! Now what? He could be the guy, and you can't prove it?"

"I'll question him. If it's him, maybe he'll slip up."

"Why even bother? You don't have anything to go to trial with—you'd never get a conviction."

"I'm telling you, it'll turn up; it's just gonna take a bit of searching."

"Yeah, well, in the meantime, would it be asking too much for you guys to keep an eye on him? We've got a lot of kids around here you know."

"Yeah, that's a good point. I'll talk to the Sarge."

"You do that."

Father Steve dropped the phone on the cradle and let out a sigh so big his shoulders heaved. Well, a lot of good that did! Maybe, just maybe, the "Sarge" would increase the patrols in the area making the kids a little safer, but he didn't really feel very confident about that.

He left his room and went down the hallway to the stairs, looked into the open door of Father Fitzgerald's room and saw Micky dusting and straightening things on a shelf. He entered quietly and touched her on the shoulder. She jumped and started to shriek, but he covered her mouth just in time. "Shhh. A boy wouldn't scream if he was scared."

She turned around and faced him, her hand on her chest, "What are you trying to do, give me a heart attack?"

"Nah. I just wanted to let you know that I'm going to the children's ward later today. You told me to tell you the next time I went so you could go with me."

"Oh, that would be great. What time? I'll have my work done here in about two hours."

He looked at his watch, "That would make it right about four. We'll have a little over an hour before it's time for them to eat dinner."

"Okay, just let me know when you're ready to leave."

"All right, I have to go out now. I'll be back for you later."

He grabbed a set of car keys, left the rectory and drove to the mall intent on buying Micky a nightgown. After walking around for fifteen minutes, he realized that he couldn't buy a woman's nightgown at his home mall; too many people knew him here. He'd hardly been able to walk ten feet without having to acknowledge someone's greeting. He got back into the car and drove to another mall almost thirty miles away. Then, just before he went inside, he removed his Roman collar and put it in his jacket pocket. He knew better than to go into Victoria's Secret; he'd just be asking for trouble, so he went directly to Macy's. There he found what he was looking for—a nice long nightgown in a size six with a matching robe and slippers. After paying for the items he took them to be gift wrapped at the customer service center.

He drove back to the rectory to pick up Micky so

they could visit the children at the hospital, and he left the package in the center of her bed before going to look for her.

There were two children from his First Communion class that were hospitalized, and he'd promised their parents that he would go pray with them and take them some Christian story books. Micky collected toys from the church's gift shop that some parishioners had donated, and he helped her carry them to the car.

On the ride to the hospital she regaled him with housecleaning horror stories ending with her lapse in judgment for letting the bug man walk all over her freshly shampooed carpets.

He watched as Micky played with the children. He laughed at her antics and the atrocious balloon animals she made for them. The children loved her and were very sorry to see her leave when their dinners arrived. On the way back he said, "You look more feminine today. Not bothering with the pretense anymore?"

"Well, there's a story to that."

"Care to share?"

"Might as well, you'll probably find out tonight anyway."

"Has something happened?"

"You could say that."

"Spill it."

"Monseigneur found out about me today."

"Really? What happened? What did he say?" he sounded very interested and at the same time, a trifle worried too.

"Well, what happened is this. I wasn't very careful about keeping my Kotex pads hidden. I started my period this morning, and I inadvertently left the box on top of my dresser when I went to class this morning. Well, Monseigneur was looking for me because he couldn't find his favorite alb that he'd asked me to iron. He came to my room to see if I was there. When I got back from class, he was standing in my room holding a Kotex pad in his hand looking a little shell shocked."

The image struck Father Steve as hilarious, and he laughed, even though he knew, that to her, it wasn't funny. Embarrassing, humiliating, and fearful, but not at all funny.

"Sorry," he said as he contained himself. "So, what did he say? He's not letting you go is he?"

"He said he was very disappointed with me, and I somehow think you're going to hear about that later, too. Then he said he had some thinking to do. I'm supposed to see him when we get back."

"Doesn't look good huh?"

"Oh, I don't know," she said with more confidence than she actually felt, "you guys aren't exactly a picnic to clean up after. I do a pretty good job keeping things clean and orderly though—maybe he will let me stay on, but I will definitely have to find another place to live. The parishioners will never go for a woman living in the rectory."

"Yeah, you've got a point there. Well, *something* will come up, never fear."

"I never do. I've learned to take the good with the bad. At least I got my tuition paid."

He smiled over at her and saw her wistful expression. "Do you need money? I have some if you do."

"No, I'm fine. My books are paid for and so are my classes. That's the only thing that really matters. *And,* I have a brand new box of Kotex. That's the other thing he's upset about."

Father Steve turned to look at her, "What are you talking about now?"

She looked down at her hands twisting in her lap, "I had them sent over with the grocery order."

"You mean you didn't pay for them?"

"No, I paid for them. I put the money on the church secretary's desk before the order was delivered, I told her I'd ordered something personal from the grocer."

"So, what's he upset about?"

"Just the idea that a large box of Kotex was delivered to the rectory. That and the fact that the order was delivered by Jedidiah Smith."

"Oh, no! Not Jedidiah!"

"Yes. The male version of Gladys Kravitz. Right about now, everybody in town probably knows that someone living in the rectory is menstruating. By tonight, everyone will know it's me." She heaved a big sigh, and he reached over and covered her hands with his large one.

The touch was electrifying, and they both sensed the fevered heat. "I'll make sure it's not printed in the bulletin."

"Gee, thanks."

"Well, here we are. Let's go see what he's got to say," he said with a grin.

"You don't seem worried at all," she said.

"Why should I be? I never mentioned your sex one way or the other, and I know that whatever happens, you'll take it like a man."

"You know, your sense of humor leaves something to be desired."

"I thought that was pretty funny myself."

"Well, don't get too full of yourself. What if he

asks you if you knew that I was a woman? What are you going to say then? Without lying, of course."

"I'll just tell him the truth, that a few weeks ago, I felt up your breast and that just last night, I saw you practically naked, and then I'll meet you out front, because we'll both be kicked out of the rectory!"

They both laughed until tears were streaming down their eyes, and they had to wait before going inside because she had the hiccups so bad that she couldn't catch her breath.

Chapter Ten

The Monseigneur had the whole afternoon to reflect on the immaculate state of the rectory as well as on the orderly way the household was running. But he'd also had the whole afternoon to field calls from several shocked parishioners, so it wasn't too much of a surprise when it was decided that Micky could keep her job but that she had to find someplace else to live. The calls went out and within a day, the Monseigneur had found a place she could live and not have to pay rent, as long as she promised to be quiet and unobtrusive and not to stay out late at night. A widow had volunteered to house Micky as a favor to the Monseigneur and in supplication to God—so things were working out.

Micky saw Father Steve the next day during class, and afterward she thanked him for the gown, robe and slippers he had left on her bed. Then that afternoon they beat each other up on the basketball court while their erstwhile teammates stared slack jawed at Micky with new eyes instead of guarding her.

Both of them were dripping sweat when they finally gave up the court. As they leaned against the mesh fence trying to catch their breath, he followed the path of a trickle of sweat as it rolled past her ear, down her throat and slipped between her cleavage. It shouldn't have been anything he'd want to lick, but for some reason, it was. He had to close his eyes against the sight.

They were both supposed to run in a charity marathon tomorrow with sixty people from the church. If this was how he reacted to her sweating, he'd better make sure he didn't hold back to run with her as he had planned.

His last prayer that night was that God keep him from being tempted by her, by her softness, by her sweetness, by her uncanny connection to his inner self.

He tossed and turned until two a.m. when he finally got up to take a cold shower. It occurred to him that he didn't turn the water on hot anymore and he knew that she was the reason. He had to make a concerted effort to avoid her. He needed his sleep and he abhorred cold showers.

In the following days when they saw each other in class he tried not to look at her. Instead he focused his attention on the other students whenever he looked up from his lecture notes. When they passed on the rectory stairs as she was doing her chamber duties, he only nodded. Twice, she cornered him into playing a game of chess and once, she stayed after class to ask a few questions. But other than that, they seldom saw each other. The guys on the basketball court were reluctant to let her play with them anymore now that they knew she was a girl, and she'd had to resign herself to the sidelines each time she'd come to play.

But with each contact with Father Steve, each meeting of the eyes, something special passed between them— something neither could name nor deny.

On Sunday, after Father Steve had celebrated the early mass, he went back to his room to change into casual clothes so he could help the youth group do some late morning planting. They had raised money by having a yard sale and now were using the proceeds to spruce up the local park.

There was a still silence in the large hall as most of the parish priests were assisting in the late Lenten mass. Father Steve had opted to do the first mass so he would be free to help the kids. As he walked through the empty hall and effortlessly ran up the staircase two steps at a time, he reveled in the quiet peace of the hall; it wasn't often that he had the whole place to himself. And for once, he was going to treat himself to a long hot shower without having to feel at all guilty about what happened when the next guy tapped into the woefully inadequate hot water heater.

Micky ran her fingers over the top of his hair brush, and then impulsively picked it up and ran it through her hair, hoping that a few of his short dark hairs would mingle into her own short blonde ones. Then she touched his toothbrush, stroking alongside the bristles that had to have brushed against his lips this very morning. As she wiped all around his sink she looked into the mirror. But she wasn't seeing her image, she was willing the mirror to show her the reflected image of him as he'd stepped out the shower this morning, his bronzed body glistening with water, the dark curling hairs all over his body, a testament to his virility. She didn't want to envision him any lower than his navel for surely God would frown upon that, but her mind filled in the blanks anyway, conjuring up a man's sacs heavy with desire for her and a penis unrealistically proportioned, she feared. She'd never seen one in its aroused state. In fact, the only ones she'd ever seen on adult men were the ones she'd seen on statues and they tended to be in the flaccid state. Heat shot through her body as she envisioned him there, watching her, raising a lone eyebrow indicating that she was way overdressed for his state of mind.

Reluctantly, she picked up the damp towels from the floor and left his bathroom. Her face brightened when she walked over to the mussed up bed. It had been many hours since he'd left it, she knew, but she still felt it for his warmth. Finding none, she picked up his pillow and immersed her face into the center of it. She was waltzing around his room, breathing in his essence as deeply as she could, when he strode into the room.

He leaned against his dresser, an arm propped on the top, and smiled as he watched her until she finally became aware of his presence. When she opened her eyes and saw him, she thought she'd die from mortification. Her face flushed as heat shot to it. She longed to suffocate herself permanently with the pillow she still held in her arms.

"Hi," was all he said as she stood stock-still and stared at him.

"H-h-hi," she stammered.

"Whatcha doin'?" he asked, feigning an innocent knowledge of her juvenile behavior.

"Uh. Ah . . . just checking to see if your pillowcase needs freshening."

"And does it?" he taunted.

"Why, yes. Yes, it does," she said quickly lowering the pillow and stripping the case from it.

He quietly closed the door. The small click of the door handle settling into the jamb drew her eyes to the now-closed door. He walked to where she stood hugging the pillow. He took the pillow from her and tossed it onto the bed, then with one hand cupped her jaw and used his thumb to lift her chin. His lips descended slowly. He pressed his mouth lightly against hers. Gently, he rubbed his lips over hers and using his lower lip and tongue, he separated her lips and inserted the slick moist tip of his tongue into her mouth. He greedily feasted on her mouth, licking and stroking all the soft, wet places until finally she could hold back no longer and she groaned aloud, "Steven, Steven . . ."

The sound of her moaning his Christian name unleashed a wanton passion, and he reached down with his other hand, grabbed her hip and pulled her tightly against his hard, tense body. Her hand flew to his face to caress his cheek as the firmness of his lips conquered her soft mouth. His hard body pressed tightly against hers, her breasts to his chest, her core meeting his. She stroked his jaw while letting her tongue assert itself and delve into his mouth. The combination of her tongue, her lips, her stroking fingers and her yielding body were too much for him; he nipped at her bottom lip and pulled away from her.

They stood looking into each other's eyes,

neither daring to say anything. At last he spoke, and his harsh words crushed her, "I'm sorry Missy, I shouldn't have done that."

"Please don't apologize for one of the best moments of my life."

"It can't happen again."

"I know."

"I want you so badly it hurts. I had to taste you, just once, but it *can't* happen again." He turned to open the door.

"Am I not suited to your taste?" she asked boldly.

He spun around to face her, "Oh, good Lord, Missy, how could you even think that! You taste wonderful. The problem is that I want to keep tasting you, all of you. Denying myself is going to be one of the hardest things I've ever had to do, so please don't make this any harder than it already is."

She walked over and boldly grabbed his crotch. "Does it *get* any harder than this?"

His pitiful groan filled the room, and he sank to his knees dragging her to the floor with him. "Missy, don't. Please, don't . . ."

But it was too late; her hand had latched onto him and was gently squeezing and caressing the large ridge that was straining to her touch. She rubbed up and down the length of him with her open palm as he strained against his zipper. Kneeling on the carpet, he massaged her breast and kissed her throat as her fingers brought him to his first climax in eight years. He sobbed into her neck as the release washed over him, and he felt his desire for her grow instead of wane. His soul felt joy for the first time in many years. When the shame that he thought he should be experiencing didn't come, he looked into her face to see love shining in her eyes.

"Oh God, I needed that," he sighed.

"I know you did," she said and she moved her hand from his groin to his shoulder. They knelt and clung to each other. Then he stood and pulled her up into his arms.

"I love you, Steven," she whispered.

"You just think you love me. I'm your teacher. I'm your priest. You're just infatuated, and I took advantage of the situation."

"That's not true, and you know it."

"Even if I weren't a priest or your teacher, I'm too old for you."

"Ten years is not that big a difference."

"It is for us. I suspect you haven't had many relationships with men, and that you don't know what it is that you're feeling."

"I haven't had *any* relationships with men. But I know you, and you don't know whether to deny what has just happened or be thrilled that it finally did. Believe what you want, Steven, but there isn't going to be any other relationships for me. If I can't have you, I don't want anybody."

He kissed her forehead, "Time will tell, you'll see. These feelings are just temporary. A few years from now, I'll be marrying you off to some young buck who won't be able to keep his hands off of you." It was killing him to say this, but he knew that he had to, for her sake. Although the thought of another man's hands roaming over her sweet body was driving him insane with jealously. But he could never let her know that. He had to send her away. He could never love a woman the way she needed a man to love her.

He looked down at his pants, "I guess I'd better take care of this."

She smiled up at him, "I like the results of my handiwork, no pun intended. But I guess it's a good thing that I'm the one who does the laundry around here. It wouldn't do to have this get around. I am glad that you're wearing underwear today, though."

"What do you mean by that?" He enjoyed the freedom of movement afforded by silk boxers, so he doubted that she could have felt whether he was wearing underwear or not just a few minutes ago.

"It's curious, but I've noticed on the days that there's a frock to send to the cleaners, there are no boxers."

He looked at his shoes and shook his head back and forth. "Learned a lot about me by doing my laundry, huh?"

"Oh, the stories I could tell about each one of you. Good thing blackmail's not my thing."

"Oh, c'mon now, I doubt that there's anything that serious in our dirty linens."

"Well, a certain priest, who shall remain nameless, has been enjoying m&m's in bed."

"What's so bad about that?"

"I happen to know that he gave up all sweets for Lent."

"Father Justy?"

"Can't say. Code of the laundress and all that."

"What else?"

"Somebody else is definitely color blind. I've yet to see any combination of colors even close, in any pair of socks."

"That's easy. That's Father Andrews, and they're probably the most expensive socks money can buy."

"No, I don't think so, yours probably are. His are handmade by his sister."

"Really?"

"Yeah, I think he gets a new pair every week. I really should suggest to him that I go through his drawers, match them up and pin them together for him."

"That would be a nice gesture."

"Yeah, well, if there's one man's drawers I'd prefer not to be in, it would certainly be his!"

He looked at her, his eyes widened and he choked as he stifled a laugh. She probably didn't know what she'd just inadvertently said, but just the same it was time to end this conversation.

"Here," he said as he handed her his pillow and a fresh pillow case from the top of the dresser, "I believe this is where you left off when I came in and interrupted you."

"A welcome interruption, I assure you," she said with a smile as she watched him go to the door and open it. He walked back through the bedroom and into his bathroom and just before closing the door, leaned out to say, "For sanity's sake, I need you to be gone when I've finished cleaning up, so please don't linger." With that, he closed the door.

She could hear him running the water in the shower as she finished remaking his bed.

So much for the idea of a hot shower, he thought, as the water beat on his chest. His body had already renewed itself, and like a magnet it was reaching out to hers. If he ever had need of a cold shower, it was now.

Chapter Eleven

The annual Greek Festival was held the following weekend, and was a major fundraiser for the parish. Even though St. Paul's was a Roman Catholic Church, not a Greek Orthodox one, they had adopted the idea of having a Greek Festival many years ago—quite a few St. Paul's parishioners had Greek origins. It was the only kind of festival not already being celebrated in this large, culturally diverse city at the time.

Friday night was the kickoff, celebrated by a special mass and communion, a feast of sausage and peppers accompanied by traditional Greek desserts, and a silent auction. Saturday would be a full day of carnival games, and Saturday night would include a dinner prepared by the Knights of Columbus, followed by a concert for the seniors and a costume toga dance for the younger set. Micky—who was now Missy again—had been asked by the set-up committee to help out, so she would be attending all the functions for free.

Friday night she sat in one of the front pews watching Father Steve perform the mass. She was awed by him and his solemnity. She'd never seen him quite as serious as this, not even when he was administering final exams. There was a sense of reverence in every movement, and she found herself almost envious of the way he handled the gold chalice and the paten. As she watched him place the single white wafer on his tongue, she was mesmerized by the sensuousness of his action. Watching his lips sip from the heavy cup was no less tantalizing, and she had to admonish herself to keep her mind on the service and its meaning. Once, his eyes found hers and she smiled, but he didn't smile back. He simply looked down at the opened book on the altar and started repeating the phrases she had heard repeated every Sunday for as long as she could remember.

On Saturday, they worked with the youth group washing what seemed to be a thousand cars, and then they both took their turns being dunked in the water tank. He was the most popular dunkee they'd ever had because he kept everyone guessing if he was going to surface after his dunking. He had incredible lungpower and usually lingered at the bottom of the tank much longer than most people could hold their breath. Twice, someone had even jumped in to 'save' him, only to be laughed at themselves when he surfaced triumphant. At Father's Steve's suggestion, Missy put a bathing suit on under her T-shirt and even though it wasn't as revealing as just her bra would have been, it did reveal enough to keep the men coming back to douse her over and over again. Their booth was by far the most profitable one that day.

Before the Knights of Columbus dinner, Missy went back to her room at the Widow Hainey's to shower and change into her costume. She'd had some help putting her costume together by two of the women who ran the thrift shop for the church. Looking into the mirror before making her way back to the church, she appraised herself. She looked quite regal in her long white, sleeveless gown edged in gold geometric bric-a-brac with rope braiding crisscrossing her breasts and wrapping around her slim waist. She'd sown all the embellishments on herself and was quite proud of how nice it looked. But more than that, she was quite pleased with how good *she* looked. The braiding accentuated her small, rounded breasts and made them appear larger than she knew them to be. The long slit up the side from her ankle to several inches above her knee flared open revealing a tantalizing glimpse of lean thigh. The gown draped beautifully from her fair shoulders to the tips of her gold-strapped sandals, and she looked so utterly feminine and sexy in it that it shocked even her. Secretly, she couldn't wait until Father Steve saw her. He was devastatingly handsome, and that was just as intimidating as his profession. But now that she had been compelled to drop her tomboy image, and dress in a feminine fashion, she had to admit that she looked quite fetching. Was it wrong to try to seduce him? She knew that it was. But she didn't really care.

Mrs. Hainey had made a wreath out of silk grape leaves for her. Now it adorned her head, her short blonde curls fanning out all around it. She didn't have any jewelry, and wasn't even sure if it would have been part of the costume for a Roman woman in the days of yore, but she did buy some lilac eye shadow and pink lipstick to complete the look. The lilac complimented the green of her eyes, and the pink of her lips made her cheeks look rosy. All in all, she thought she'd done a pretty fantastic job of turning the tomboy Micky into Venus, the seductive goddess of love and beauty.

Father Steve was in a counseling session during

most of the dinner hour. He'd had an urgent phone call from one of the parish youths and had agreed to meet the boy right away. It seemed that the eighteen-year old youth and his seventeen-year-old girlfriend were having a crisis in their four-year relationship. He wanted to marry her but her parents refused, saying they would not give their permission until she had her diploma.

A smart decision, Father Steve told him.

That wasn't the real problem, the boy said. The real problem was that his girlfriend wanted to be a virgin on their wedding night.

Again, Father Steve smiled and nodded, so where was the problem? That sounded like a wise decision, and he admired the girl for sticking to her guns.

The problem, was that the girl had agreed to perform oral sex on him, but she needed someone to tell her it was all right in the eyes of the church. Also, she needed someone to tell her exactly how to go about doing it so she wouldn't make herself sick. She'd overheard some girls talking about how it had made them puke all over their boyfriends laps the first time they'd tried it.

"Let me get this straight, Hank," Father Steve said as he unconsciously smoothed the hair at his temples. "You want me to tell Amy that it's okay for her to go down on you, and then you want me to *tell her how to do it so she doesn't gag and embarrass herself?*"

"No, no, of course not." It did sound ridiculous now that he heard it said out loud. It had been a mistake coming here, Hank thought. A huge mistake.

Father Steve looked over at the abashed young

man and his sympathies kicked in, "What have you been doing up 'til now to uh . . . alleviate things."

"Necking and dry humping, only it hasn't been quite that dry," Hank said sheepishly.

"And for her?"

"I've diddled her and attempted oral sex on her, but I don't think she's comfortable with it. And probably won't be until you say it's okay."

"Ahh, Hank. What to say, what to say? I know this is a hard time for you. No pun intended there," he said with a smile, "but what's important to her had better be important to you, or you're setting yourself up for a lot of trouble later."

"Yeah, I know. Why do you think I'm here?"

"I think you're here for me to tell you both to go ahead."

Hank grinned broadly, "And will you?"

Father Steve flashed a sideways smile and shook his head, "No, I won't."

"Why not?"

"Because it's not my decision. Some people don't think oral sex is proper even when they're married. That's a very individual thing. And I don't think you're going to buy yourself much time with this maneuver. Putting yourselves in the situation where you're experiencing that kind of heated passion will leave you powerless to control yourselves. The thing that you don't want to happen, the thing that you're trying so hard to avoid, may just come about because your guard will be down. If she feels so strongly about being a virgin for you on your wedding night, she may not forgive you for taking that away from her. Having oral sex will just cloud the issue. If you can't abstain, maybe you should talk about setting a firm wedding date and finding some other activities to get involved in. Try not to be alone with each other so much. Instead of going parking, go bowling. Find some people in the community who need help with their houses, trade hours of painting now for hours of babysitting later. Because once you two do tie the knot, that's going to be the next problem, finding the time to be alone again."

"Yeah, I guess you're right, Father. That's a good idea. I'll stick it out a little longer, if I can." He stood to leave.

"Hank?" Father Steve was leaning back in his chair tapping a pencil against the desk and looking up at him.

"Yeah?"

"When it is time and you want her to do something, be gentle. Teach her yourself; show her all the places you most want her to touch. Explain what it does to you, and why it would feel so good if she would just try it one time. Once she sees how much joy it gives you when she does what you show her, she'll come to like it. Just take it slow and make sure you take your time with her. And if you can't spend at least fifteen minutes loving her before you enter her, then don't expect her to do anything special for you."

"I'll remember that. Thanks, Father Steve."

"You're welcome."

Long after Hank left, Father Steve sat studying the wall in one of the downstairs offices. He hoped he'd given the boy the right advice. But one thing was for sure; all this talk about necking, petting and oral sex was creating control problems for *him*. Abstaining until your wedding day was one thing, abstaining for the rest of your life was another.

Chapter Twelve

After all this time, he still didn't know if this was the right course for him. He'd been a priest for several years now and still wasn't sure that this was what he was supposed to be. He had done what his father had wanted—what his father had insisted on. But now that his father was gone, did it really matter any more?

He had never experienced the thrill of accomplishment, the dedication to the cause, the excitement of finally achieving his Roman collar. He thought back to his graduation day, the day he and his classmates graduated from the seminary, the day the sacrament of ordination had been celebrated. His ordination hadn't really been all that special to him. He knew that he had never wholly accepted the sacrament; that he had never really felt as one with the church like he should have.

Although he fully understood and earnestly performed all the functions of a priest, he never really felt God's peace about it. He felt as if he was just standing in and doing a job he'd prepared for, instead of feeling awed and honored to be performing the holy rites. He was a good priest though, he knew that. He did a lot for the community, especially for the disadvantaged.

Almost on his own he'd wiped out the gang influence in some of the poorer neighborhoods. There were hardly ever fights anymore between the ethnic youths in their section of the city. But even though he loved certain aspects of his job, such as teaching and counseling, he often hated the way the options regarding his own life had been taken away from him the day he'd put on that stiff white collar. Mostly, because he knew he hadn't made the decision for himself.

He knew that it had only been because his father had begged him until he was completely worn down. Begged him to spend his life devoted to praying for the souls of his beloved mother and sister, and then years later, his father's.

And now look at him. Here he was, inheriting a lot of money that he hadn't even known existed, sitting in his office incredibly aroused from impure thoughts brought on by his conversation with Hank, and by a strange quirk of fate, he was father confessor to the man who had murdered his mother and sister. And, he thought, that just possibly, he might be falling for one of his students. A student who had looked especially delectable today in a wet T-shirt, even with a bathing suit on underneath it.

He forced himself out of the oversized leather desk chair and headed to the fellowship hall to grab a bite of dinner and to join in the festivities.

How it happened, he didn't know, but he ended up in line next to Mrs. Reynolds and was therefore obligated to join her for dinner when he was invited. He listened to her banter as he shoveled in his food, anxious to have an excuse to get up and move away from her when he spotted Missy on the other side of the room. She was talking to a group of women, and when they parted from standing in front of her, his breath caught in his throat. *Dear God, she was stunning.*

He managed to swallow the piece of bread he'd been chewing without choking, but his eyes never left her. He drank her in, filling his senses with her. He didn't know when he'd ever seen a lovelier woman, and it shook him to the core to realize how badly he wanted her.

"She's lovely," Rita said as she followed his gaze.

Quickly, he turned back to her, feigning confusion. "What?"

"She's lovely, I said. And to think, just a few days ago, we all thought she was a boy," she said snidely.

He smiled to himself, he remembered how she'd stroked and caressed Missy's arm that night when Missy was polishing the rectory's silver. "She's a sweet kid," he said.

"Oh, I'm sure she is. Funny, she doesn't seem to have a boyfriend, though. A girl that pretty ought to have several don't you think?"

The thought of Missy having boyfriends wasn't a welcome one. "She's only interested in her education right now. She's an excellent student."

"Oh, I'm sure she is," she said with a smirk. "I'm sure she is."

"Well, I think I'll go mingle. Nice sitting with you, Rita."

"Any time, Father," she said with a big smile, as she looked him up and down, her eyes lingering purposefully on his crotch. "Any time at all."

It was several minutes before he could make his way around to where Missy was. When he stood in front of her, he shook his head in disbelief and smiled,

"You look absolutely beautiful."

She beamed and gave a shallow curtsy, "Thank you. Do you know who I am?"

"Missy?" he asked.

"No, silly. Greek-goddess wise."

"Oh. Helen?"

She laughed and his stomach clenched. What a joy she was.

"Do I look like I have a face that could launch ships?"

Actually right now, she truly did. She was launching him all right, launching him clear into outer space. "I don't have a boat, but if I did, you could certainly launch it."

"That's very sweet. But, I'm not Helen; I'm Venus, goddess of love and beauty. See, here are my apples." She tossed three golden apples up into the air and juggled them expertly before catching all three again.

"Apples?"

"Venus led Hippomenes to a tree where she told him to pluck three apples, the apples helped him beat Atalanta in a foot race, where he won her as his bride. But he forgot to thank Venus so she changed them both into lions that only the moon goddess could tame."

"Man, you just can't trust a woman when it comes to apples, can you?" he said. She knew he was alluding to Eve. They both laughed, and he looked deeply into her eyes. "I need to talk to you. Can you meet me in twenty minutes down by the gate in the old garden past the cemetery?"

Her eyes filled with concern. "Sure. That's a long, spooky walk though. Everything all right?"

"I just need to talk to you. Privately." *I just need*

to be with you, he thought. *I know it's wrong, but Lord help me, I can't help myself.*

He was waiting for her twenty minutes later when she approached the old, creaky gate. Several times during the last few minutes, he'd almost turned and left. *This was ludicrous! What was he doing?* He saw her walking toward him and his heart soared. He opened the gate for her and walked with her into the oldest section of the garden, an area filled with gnarled oaks and large gray tombstones, some of them so large that you could hide behind them without crouching. The church was having renovations done to some of the older tombstones, and this part of the cemetery was posted off limits due to the haphazard way the construction crews were digging up the ground. He took her hand and led her over to a tall, smooth headstone reflecting the moonlight and creating a pool of light for them to stand in.

"What's on your mind?" she asked.

"Would you ever have premarital sex?" he blurted out.

She blinked and raised her eyebrows at his question, then countered him with, "What makes you think I haven't already?"

"I just don't think that you have. Have you?"

"No. No, I haven't. Is there a particular reason you're asking me this?"

"Yes."

When he didn't elaborate, she thought for a minute. "Yes, I think that I might." She was thinking about making love with him. Yes, she would definitely have premarital sex with him, she'd have any kind of sex with him that he wanted. More firmly she stated, "Yes, if the circumstances were right, I would."

"Even though it's a sin?"

"Yes."

"Oral?"

She stared at him her eyes wide, her mouth agape. "Pardon?"

Oh God. What had he done? Did she even know what he was talking about? Did she think he was asking her for it? "I mean would oral sex be less sinful to you than the conventional way?"

She cleared her throat and started to speak but nothing came out, so she tried again. "I'm not sure. I only know what I've read in books about it. I wouldn't be against learning, though. Just why are you asking me this?"

"I don't exactly know now," he said, and then he actually cursed and walked away. He'd wanted to know if he'd advised the kids properly, but now all he was doing was thinking about her, thinking about her kneeling between his legs . . .

He got as far as the first cluster of tombstones before coming back. He had so much on his mind now. But maybe, just maybe, she could help. If he could just stop thinking about how lovely and innocent she was long enough to confide in her and ask her opinion.

"What if you promised someone not to reveal a secret, but every waking moment you agonized over it, wanting so very much to tell? To scream it actually."

"Who did you promise that you wouldn't tell?"

"God."

"That's what I thought." A few moments passed in silence, then she whispered, "A confession." It wasn't even a question.

"Yeah."

"That night, the night you taught me how to

play chess."

He nodded.

"You can't tell."

"I know."

"What's more, it's keeping you from falling in love, isn't it?"

"Pardon?" he said as he spun back around from his pacing to look at her. God, she was beautiful. The moonlight was surrounding her like a soft halo.

She pushed off from the stone and walked a few yards to a large tree. Leaning against the trunk she said, "When you have something that big that you're hiding, you can't share your life. There's just too much that's not yours anymore."

"How do you know it's big?" he persisted, following her.

"Because it's the elephant that's between us."

"Just what does that mean?" he asked, totally perplexed.

"You've got issues, big issues. But they all boil down to whether to stay a priest or give your life to God."

"If I stay a priest, I *am* giving my life to God!"

"Not if He doesn't want it that way."

"What the hell are you talking about?" He was getting agitated now and he really didn't know why. *How could she know these things about him? And what was that about focusing on falling in love?*

"Did it ever occur to you that maybe, just maybe, He wants you to spend your life with a woman, raising a family?"

God, just how perceptive was this woman? He walked over to where she stood and cupped her cheek. Softly he said, "Since I found out you're a woman it has occurred to me every single minute of every single day."

He lowered his head, took her mouth softly with his, and slowly threaded his fingers through her curls, now loose at her temple.

"My love," she whispered, and he groaned into her mouth before savagely pulling her to him.

Their embrace was fevered and passionate, and deliciously wicked because they both knew it was wrong, wrong for them to be here like this. But wrong was making it feel oh . . . so . . . right, and so incredibly wonderful. Her soft breasts were pushed into the hard plains of his chest and his thigh was pressed tight against her mons.

He couldn't stop now. He had to keep her body close to his. He had to feel her soft, yielding flesh molding into his hard, tense muscles. His hand splayed wide on her back, slid down so he could grab her buttocks and pulled her tightly against his aroused manhood.

The heat of their bodies was almost too much to bear. As his tongue delved into her mouth, scorching her and sending flames of desire shooting through her, his fingers on her backside pressed her pulsing femininity against his maleness. She lifted her pelvis to meet his thrusts and they both moaned with ecstasy as their gyrations ignited them even more.

His lips slid from her eager mouth to a vein pulsing at her jaw, then on to a delicate whorl above her earring. The blood in her veins spiked with reaction to the touch of his tongue running along the creases, and molten desire flooded through her. He kissed her and murmured, "We can't, we can't, we can't." But despite his words, he never slowed his downward descent.

"No . . . no . . . we can't," she agreed wrapping

her arms around his neck and lifting her head, exposing the long column of her throat.

His lips and tongue worked their way back, thoroughly delighting in her delicate ear, yet he took the detour she was offering and lovingly kissed his way down to her collarbone where his hand prepared the way by baring her shoulder. His other hand searched out the end of the gold braid at her waist and gently tugged. The cord unraveled, and the crossed constraints holding the top of her gown up loosened and fell. Her low moan encouraged him and his fingers slid the fabric from her shoulder to her elbow. He tucked his fingers under the thin material covering her breasts and gently pulled. With a gasp, she realized she was naked from the waist up.

His hand moved to cup her left breast. He allowed some separation so he could step back to look at her and these newly uncovered treasures. The groan of his extreme pleasure sent heat racing through her while her nipples reacted to the coolness of the night air. A plumping sensation she had never experienced before generated a heavy feeling and made her less self conscious of her small breasts.

"Beautiful," he whispered reverently. His eyes caressed her for several long moments before his mouth lowered to taste a small budded tip. The second his tongue touched her, she felt a heavy weight descend to her lower body and desire pooled in her. It was as if the gravity of the earth had increased; her breasts felt heavier and grew dense, her womb contracted. Desire raged out of control. It was all she could do to remain standing. She leaned back against the tree, only vaguely aware of the rough bark pressing into the smooth skin of her back. His fingertips closed around the nipple of her other breast, and she moaned her satisfaction.

He traced his tongue between her breasts and moved his mouth to her other breast. He suckled on the tip, pulling it away from her body with his lips. Her soft gasp pleased him but also reminded him of her innocence. "We can't do this," he murmured softly as he stepped away from her again. His hands were still on her breasts, his fingers moving over her, cupping her and gently tugging on her nipples while his eyes devoured her. She closed her eyes, arched her head back and moaned, "Yes, we can. You can't leave me like this."

He was instantly reminded of the troubled youth he'd counseled this afternoon and knew that if he expected him to hold back, then he must do likewise.

"No. We really can't," he said and moved his hands to her shoulders and stepped between her parted thighs. He pulled her close. With her breasts up against his chest, he moved his hands from her shoulders to her back, lifting her away from the tree. He rubbed her back in large circles and pressed her closer. Finally, his hands searched out her straps and he lifted them up her arms to her shoulders.

"Please . . . " she begged.

"I can't. I'm a priest. The Vatican frowns on this kind of thing. And, I'm your teacher. I could go to jail for what I just did."

"No, you couldn't. I'm over eighteen and I'd never press charges."

"Well, at any rate, it's unethical. Next thing I know, you'll be insisting on getting an 'A' in my course." She could hear the wry humor in his voice and sensed his smile as he kissed the top of her shoulder.

Indignantly, she countered him with, "I deserve an 'A' in your class and you know it!"

"See. See what I mean?"

"I'm your best student, you can't deny that."

"If I was grading on the curve, your curves would pass any test I could come up with," he said as his hand fell to her hip.

"You say the nicest things, but I really need you," she breathed.

"I can't."

"Please, please. Just touch me. Feel me there. Please."

He groaned at her words, but was unable to pull himself away when she took his hand and inserted it between the long slit of her skirt, and placed it high on her thigh.

He slid his hand slowly up her leg, dragging the material of her gown higher as it draped over the back of his hand. When his hand reached her hip, he hesitated for just a moment before letting his hand follow the line of her panties. With his palm flat against her abdomen, he felt her smooth, warm skin and caressed her navel with his thumb. His fingers grazed the lacy edge of her panties, then before he could talk himself out of it, he quickly inserted his hand inside. They both sighed when his splayed hand reached her soft tufts of hair. He knew it was blonde like the hair on her head just by the feel of it; the springy hairs were incredibly soft and fine. His fingers toyed gently with the soft curls, and before she could prepare herself for his touch, his long middle finger dove down and separated her cleft. "Oh, sweetheart," he murmured, "you are so wet." His finger slid back and forth in the soft, velvety channel of her womanhood. He enjoyed the feel of her smooth, silky wet folds. "So wet, so very, very wet," he repeated hoarsely.

His finger tunneled into her shallow opening. He shoved it deep, luxuriating in the feel of her damp hair against his palm as his finger delved inside her throbbing flesh. As he buried his finger up to its last knuckle in her warm moist cavity, his foremost thought was that he couldn't remember a woman ever being so ready for him, so eager to accept him into her body. He repeatedly thrust his finger into her, marveling at her velvety slickness before retreating and sliding it forward to press against her swollen and throbbing frontal node. With a few knowing touches, he caused her to tremble against his fingers. Under his constant, sure pressure, her body arched and spasmed against his marauding thumb. When she came, he gently cupped her as her body slumped into his large hand. He remained holding her like that until her breathing slowed. His breathing was shallow yet both were softly panting. After a few quiet moments, they both became aware that he was still cupping her. He gently squeezed her mound, then reluctantly removed his hand from her. He kissed her on the tip of her nose. Her sensitized skin trembled when his fingers grazed her belly as he removed his hand from her panties.

"Ohhh..." she moaned through pursed lips. "That was absolutely incredible . . . I never knew . . . "

"Never?"

"Never."

"What was wrong with the guys in your high school?"

"I was a good Catholic girl, remember?"

He smiled broadly, "You're still a good Catholic girl."

He straightened her skirt and smiled down at her, "My sweet, innocent Micky." He dragged a finger down her jaw line. "And to think, I once thought you were a man."

"I'm glad you found out otherwise."

He leaned down and took her lips with his. Tenderly, he plied them with soft nips until his own passion nearly undid him. "Aaargh," he said and set her away from him. "We cannot do this! Being near you is driving me crazy, but I cannot have you. As much as I want to take you, we both know that I *cannot*."

She traced his moist lips with her fingertip. "I know," she whispered. "I know."

"C'mon, we'd better get back. We've been gone too long already."

"Do you think anybody suspects?" she asked.

"I don't think so, but that doesn't matter. Someone has to be looking for Venus, the goddess of love and beauty, and it certainly wouldn't do either of us any good if we were discovered out here alone. He took her hand, pulled her away from the tree and squeezed her fingers tightly before releasing them. "I meant what I said. You look absolutely stunning tonight, I'm sure you're being missed by a whole slew of guys who are just finding out that Micky is Missy, a fascinating, beautiful woman."

He lifted her hand and kissed her fingertips before releasing it. "And by the way, I did not like your answer about premarital sex. From now on if a man asks you what I asked you, the answer is 'No!' " But even the thought of her having a legitimate union with another man turned his stomach sour.

He was still burning with desire for her. The illicit release he sought in her body, the culmination he continued to deny himself, was a constant reminder of his unsuitability as her suitor . . . as her lover. Though desire for her pulsed through his veins, his mind reeled with the consequences of satisfying such an urge. It would not be just a sin, although that would be bad enough, it would be disrespectful to her. She was a virgin and deserved to be loved by a man who would marry her, then make her his on their marriage bed, on their wedding night. Not by a man who had promised to love only God; a man who had agreed to put aside his mortal self to bring honor to God, a man who had taken Christ as his bride.

So why did it hurt so much to turn her aside? Why was it so difficult to let her go, he asked himself. Surely, if God sanctioned this feeling he had for her, he would not be experiencing this kind of agony and denial. Or was he wrong? Was he, as she had implied, denying the wrong thing? They walked in silence past the stony, shadowed statues of the disciples. Peter would not be happy with him, neither would Paul, Luke . . . Matthew . . . Mark . . .

By the time they left the garden and saw the lights coming through the windows of the hall, they had cooled down and become detached in their thinking. Without a word being said, he fell back and watched her walk into the church. He allowed her several minutes to enter the hall and join a group, before following several minutes later.

Later that night, when he returned to his room after helping clean up, he found a small, gray, stuffed elephant propped against his pillow. He had seen Missy win a prize at the basketball booth set up in the hall but hadn't seen what she had selected. How like her to find a subtle way to remind him of what they had talked about tonight. As if he would forget what they had talked about, or what they had done.

Chapter Thirteen

When Father Steve returned from a meeting with the altar boys he had a phone message from Rita Reynolds. The message said it was urgent that he call her. He went to his downstairs office and phoned her. What in the world did that woman want now, he asked himself as he punched in the numbers on the message slip.

"Hello?"

"Rita?"

"Father Steve! How good of you to call right back."

"Your message says urgent. What's the matter?"

"I need to talk to you. In person. Here."

"Rita," he said with a veiled hint of exasperation in his voice, "What's going on? Why do I need to come over there?"

"Well, you don't really. I just thought you'd rather talk about what happened in the graveyard here rather than over the phone."

"The graveyard?" he asked, a touch of confusion in his voice.

"Yes, the graveyard. You know, down the path,

through the rusty gates to the ancient tombstones and gnarly old trees. There's lots of hiding places back there, lots of places for secret meetings, if you know what I mean."

He knew exactly what she meant. Damn! They'd had a voyeur, and of course it would have been Rita.

"I'll be right over."

"I thought you'd prefer that," she said and hung up the phone.

Twenty minutes later, Father Steve was sitting in Rita Reynolds' living room, on her pristine sofa, his elbows balanced on his knees, hands clasped together in a loose grip, his fingertips drumming against each other while he stared down at the carpet between his knees. "So, you saw?" he asked, already resigned to the confrontation and what it could mean.

"What does she have that I don't have?" Rita asked in a soft whisper that almost came off as a sob.

He looked up and met her eyes as she sat on the love seat across from him. "My heart. I think I'm in love with her, Rita."

The grimace on her face reminded him of Cruella DeVille as her overly-madeup features contorted to this unwelcome news. A look of astonishment changed to one of total disgust. Then she showed her true feelings of disdain by spitting out, "Love! How could you love *her*?" She was aghast with this revelation, and her composure showed it as she stood and paced, her hands trembling.

"I'm not sure exactly how it happened, it just did." He stood to meet her as she turned and paced back. They stared at each other for several uncomfortable moments, neither saying anything, both absorbing the words he had said.

Finally, Father Steve took her hands in his, "Rita," he said, "I know what I'm asking is not in compliance with what the church would expect of you in this type of situation, but do you think you could sit on this until I've decided how to handle it?"

She simply stared back at him, her mouth still agape from his revelation. Finally, the inevitability of it all seeped into her, and she lowered her head and nodded. "Yeah. On one condition."

"And what's that?"

"I want one kiss. One kiss like the ones you gave her. I want to feel what it's like to be kissed by a man like you, to be desired by a man like you."

"But I don't desire you," he said bluntly. When she cringed from his tone he knew he could have said it in a less caustic way.

"Then I suggest you fake it, because that's the deal," she said with a pathetic smile. "That's my condition for silence—take it or leave it."

"I'll take it," he bit out as his left hand reached out and roughly drew his fingers through the hair at her temple, his palm cupping her ear as he drew her close. His roughness was a good cover for his contempt, but she felt his touch as she needed to feel it—as if he was full of pent up, frustrated desire.

"And don't you dare gyp me," she murmured when his lips descended to hers.

His lips caressed hers, and he tried to feign a passion that wasn't there by pressing his mouth roughly against hers. Eagerly, she opened her mouth to his and coaxed his tongue inside. He should have known she wouldn't be satisfied without the French aspect of a kiss, so he dutifully chased her tongue around the interior of her mouth, timidly touching her teeth before withdrawing it and ending the kiss. He felt tawdry, and ashamed of himself. He felt something else too, guilt for his betrayal—not for his vows—but for his betrayal of Missy. He had been disloyal to her and that pained him.

He pulled away from Rita and stood back to look down into her face. Her eyes filled with tears, and she quickly turned away from him.

Never in her life had she wanted to be somebody else. But now, she wanted to be Micky or Missy or whatever the hell her name was. She wanted to be the woman who would probably be the recipient of kisses like that for the rest of her life.

"Your secret's safe with me," she muttered and briskly walked him to the door.

"Thank you, Rita."

She looked up into his eyes, and he saw the wetness shimmering there, "I knew you'd be good. I just didn't know how good. She'd better take good care of you. If she doesn't, you know where to find me."

"Rita, it's not a given that I'll be leaving the priesthood."

"Don't kid yourself. I've seen you around her. Whether you know it or not she's become the focal point of your life. God's running a close second now and you know it. You can torture yourself by denying your feelings for her, but it won't change anything. In the end, you'll surrender. I just wish it was me you were surrendering to."

"I'm sorry."

"Yeah, me too."

The next time Father Steve saw Missy was in class. As soon as he walked into the classroom and faced the students, his eyes searched and found hers. He was instantly oblivious to all the other students whose eyes were on him. Finally, he turned away to shuffle the papers on the podium. Throughout his long lecture he was aware of her eyes on him, and when he handed copies of a quiz to the recipient of each front row seat for them to pass back, his eyes met hers again. She smiled, and he had to close his eyes to keep from acknowledging her. But while the class had their heads bent in concentration over their tests, he focused his eyes on her. His eyes drank her in. From the short blonde curls growing out in a sexy Meg Ryan style, to her hunched shoulders hiding her small bosom, to her well-formed legs and trim little feet tucked under her. She was adorable, and he was most definitely smitten. He became incredibly turned on as she sat there nibbling on the end of her pencil while holding her head up with her hand under her chin, and studying the paper in front of her.

She was one of the first ones to finish. He watched her as she bent over and placed her pencil in her book bag. He looked at her chest and to the slight shadowing between her breasts. How could breasts that small be so enticing? During class he was privy to a bevy of buxom bosoms constantly poking out of all manner of tops, but that didn't faze him in the least. And Mrs. Reynolds' bountiful duo showcased in provocative blouses did absolutely nothing for him, tucked away or blatantly bared, he was not at all affected.

Missy sat up and started to stretch, then her eyes met his, and she self-consciously abbreviated her actions. Even she knew that stretching was accentuating her breasts and putting her pert nipples in his direct line of vision. He remembered her nipples well. They had been incredibly responsive to his touch.

Father Steve abruptly turned and faced the rest of the class. "Time's up. Pass your papers to the front of the class. And remember your term paper is due tomorrow. Tomorrow during class, not tomorrow before midnight at the rectory," he said directing his comments at a young man in the first row who had a sheepish expression on his face. The rest of the class laughed and rose to leave.

Father Steve collected the papers, making sure he had everyone's, then looked up to find her. She was near the door. A male student who had transferred in for the spring semester had corralled her. He was quite good-looking and he knew it. He was smiling down at her while she idly twisted and tucked a stray curl behind her ear. Over and over again, she fidgeted with it and Father Steve realized that she was nervous, nervous because the new student was apparently asking her out. She lowered her lashes, and looked beneath them to where he was standing at the front of the class, stacking the quiz papers.

His gut clenched and he felt like he had been punched, but tried not to show any emotion as he quickly turned and shoved the papers into his briefcase. When he looked up again, they were gone. Probably arm-in-arm, him offering to carry her books, if they even did that kind of thing anymore. Jealously leapt through him, and he had to bite his tongue to keep from muttering the foul words that were erupting in him. Didn't she know he was only interested in one thing? That he wasn't interested in studying with her, watching her eat a burger, or showing off his athletic prowess in front of her. He was interested in bedding her, putting his body into hers—plain and simple. The young man was seeing a hot female that he had passed on when he'd thought her a man. Now he was making up for lost time by moving in before anybody else could.

Father Steve was amazed at how quickly he had developed such strong negative feelings toward this young man, a man that he hardly knew—all because he was interested in his girl. *His girl?* What the hell was he thinking? He grabbed his briefcase and stalked out of the room, slamming the classroom door behind him so hard that the glass rattled.

Later that night while grading the test papers, he came across Missy's. At the very bottom she had written in her delicate script, "I'd better get an 'A.' " He didn't even bother checking her paper, he took his red pen and scrawled "A+" at the top of the paper, then smiled as he laid it on top of the pile.

The only thing that dulled his lightness of being was the thought that flashed through his mind when he saw the picture of his mother and father on top of his dresser on the other side of his room: I can't love her and have her in my life, just as they couldn't love each other and live happily ever after. The man who had destroyed their happiness was in this city and as attracted to Missy as he was, he could not forget that there was a monster out there who could revert back to his evil ways at any time.

Walking back from dinner at an all night diner, he was almost knocked off his feet by three young girls wobbling in their high heels, tugging at their short

skirts, and chatting on their cell phones. Their shrieking voices carried as he recovered and gained the sidewalk again. He stood stupefied as he listened to their phone conversations.

"Can you imagine, the second date and he wanted me to suck his cock! He'd hardly even kissed me! Hell no! Maybe tonight though. I'm meeting him in an hour. I'm undecided. But I'm on my period so I know he's not going to be fucking me, that's for sure."

"Mom, I need thirty-five dollars, and I need it now. Unless you want me to get pregnant. I took my last pill this morning. Yeah, yeah. I know. Don't tell Pa. Thanks. I'll come get it now and then go to the Pharmacy. I'm meeting Randy when he gets off work at eleven. Ma! You know I won't be home by midnight, don't even suggest it. I'll be home by one, two at the latest. I know, I know, it's a school night, but nobody gets home by midnight."

"You did not see me kissing Jason at Lila's party! I wasn't even there for Chrissakes! Johnnie! Don't say that! I am not a whore! I wasn't even there! You saw someone else. Even drunk, I wouldn't kiss Jason! Johnnie, please, please believe me. Meet me now; I'll make you happy Johnnie, I promise. Please, meet me now. I'll show you that Jason means nothing to me, absolutely nothing. I'm hot for you baby, just you. Okay, okay. I'll be there. Wait for me Johnnie. I'll do you good. I'll ride you hard just the way you like. Un huh. Yeah . . . yeah, okay, you can put it in both places. I'm on my way."

He watched as all three snapped their phones shut, gave each other quick air kisses and hugs and then went their separate ways, fingers flying on their keyboards as their heels made staccato noises *on the pavement.*

Sluts! Every one of them. Younger and younger they spread their thighs for salivating, pimple-faced jocks who wielded power over them solely because the girls outnumbered the boys. Each girl in her quest to secure herself a mate was using her body as a fertile trap. It sickened him. Where were the virgins? Were there no more virgins in the high schools anymore? Did no woman wait to surrender in the marriage bed? There must be one, somewhere there must be one pure, untouched angel. He would find her. And she would smile sweetly when he entered her.

What was he saying? He could not do that anymore. He could not defile a woman that way. Even if he could find a virgin—he could not. He could not. But his palms itched and his throat ran dry and his shriveled penis leapt.

Chapter Fourteen

On Saturday, Father Steve spied Missy in the nursery as he walked by on his way back to the rectory after teaching a Catechism class. He stopped in the doorway and watched her for a few minutes as she daintily hung decorated blown eggs from pastel ribbons on a silver Christmas tree. He looked her up and down, trying to find fault with her, some little thing he could use to convince himself that she was not for him. But he could not. To him, she was just perfect; beautiful in a natural way and totally without pretense.

She must have sensed someone watching her, because she turned and saw him and gave him a big smile that melted his heart. "Hey, come see what we're doing," she said as she picked up another egg carton from the table. It was then that he noticed two preschoolers on the other side of the tree.

He put his hands in his pockets and walked into the room, "Isn't that a Christmas tree?"

"Well, it was, four months ago. Now it's an Easter tree. Right guys?"

The kids chorused "Yeaaah," as they hung fragile paper maché ornaments.

"We thought we could take this old silver artificial

tree, decorate it with cute little bunnies, fluffy chicks, and some fancy eggs. Then on Easter morning, we're going to hang all those," she pointed to a felt bulletin board with flocked religious symbols stuck to it, "eat carrot cookies and turn on the wheel to watch the color show. If we can get the wheel to work that is. So far I've only been able to get the tree to spin, not the color wheel."

"Well here, let me take a look at it." He walked over to the color wheel which was sitting in several pieces on a low table.

"Where'd you get all this stuff anyway?"

"Mrs. Hainey's attic. You would not believe the cool stuff she's got up there. Good . . . old . . . stuff," she said with a smile as she reached to hang an egg. Her shirt came away from the waistband of her skimpy skirt and he watched as the bare expanse of her midriff elongated, giving him quite an eyeful of her smooth torso. It was all he could do to keep his hands from reaching for her. Just as she stepped down and away to admire the way the egg looked, two mothers came into the room to claim their kids.

"Oh, what a beautiful tree," one exclaimed.

"Missy, how clever," the other one said, as she bent low to scoop up her child.

"Wait 'til you see it on Easter Sunday with the color wheel," she said with a smile. "If Father Steve can get it working."

"Oh, I'll get it working," he said, "either that or it'll be in a lot more pieces."

They all chuckled, and then he and Missy were alone in the quiet little nursery room. It was Saturday afternoon, and everyone had left the school except them.

"You're so clever," he mimicked with an endearing smile.

"And you're so good with your hands," she said, indicating the light he was working on, but they both knew what she really meant.

"Missy . . . " he admonished.

"I know. Don't go there." After a few moments of silence, she started to tidy up. "Do you think you can fix it?"

"Yes, in fact, I think it's fixed. Let's plug it in and see." He set the wheel a few feet away from the tree, aimed it toward the middle and then plugged the cord in. "Okay, here we go," he said and flicked on the light switch. Different color panels took their turn in front of the light bulb and the colors reflected and swirled all over the tree.

"Beautiful," she said with a radiant smile as she looked up at it. "It's just beautiful."

He looked at her and smiled at her sincere pleasure. *She* was beautiful, just beautiful.

"Let's see what it looks like with the lights off," she said and flicked the light switch. The walls and the ceiling came to life with the flowing colors. "Awesome. The kids will really love this."

What kid wouldn't love this woman with her sense of awe and wonder in the commonplace little things? "Looks like a Christmas tree we had once," he said wistfully, "only where you have the eggs, my mom had hung shiny blue balls."

"You're sounding a bit melancholy there. Memories of long ago holidays making you homesick?"

"I've been homesick for over eight years."

"So, why don't you go home?"

"I can't. There's no home to go home to and nobody there even if there was." He thought of his mother and sister, how they were murdered, and the fact that the murderer was here in town, free.

"Oh, I'm sorry. I didn't know. You have no family at all?"

"None. But I have wonderful childhood memories—they sustain me."

They stood there in the semi-darkness looking at the tree catching the light from the spinning color wheel as it splashed the silver tinsel with radiant jewel tones.

Missy sighed and whispered, "I remember Christmas mornings when my mom and dad would make me stand at the top of the stairs until my mom could get her camera ready. She always had to have a picture of my reaction when I saw all the presents under the tree."

"And they were all for you, right? You were an only child?"

"Yes," she said. "They told me God only wanted my mother to have one child, that the others would be too sick to play with me, so they told God to keep them in heaven with him so he could play with them. Later I found out that my mom had to have a hysterectomy right after I was born. She had hemorrhaged so badly during childbirth that they couldn't stop the bleeding. I think that was the start of the depression that eventually caused her to take her own life."

"And Christmas just isn't the same anymore, is it?" He said in a husky voice, and she wasn't sure he was referring to her Christmases or his.

"No. I haven't had a good Christmas, one than meant anything more than a nice long holiday for a long, long time."

He looked at her, "Doesn't the fact that it's the birthday of the Christ child mean anything to you anymore?"

"Well, yeah. But I'm not convinced that his birthday was in December. I think it happened in May. That's the prettiest month there is, and I think God would have wanted that for his only son. Christmas is too commercialized. I like to celebrate Christ's birth in the spring, when everything comes back to life."

"You're a weird duck, you know that?"

"Yeah. I know. So what about you, what do you get out of Christmas?"

"To be honest, the Christmas season is so busy around here that all I get is overworked. By the time the holiday actually arrives I usually end up spending the day in bed, sick with something a parishioner gave me."

"Nice Christmas present."

"Yeah. Not at all like the ones I used to get."

"Tell me about your Christmases. What were they like when you were a child?"

"Umm," he said as he sat down on a low wooden table a few feet away from the tree so he could look over at it as it turned and sparkled. "Let's see, there was always lots of good food and lots of company. Cards taped all over the front door, singing around the piano, a big train set under the tree, and presents with reindeer names."

"Presents with reindeer names?"

"Yeah. My mom got tired of me and my sister shaking everything to see what it was. She hated it when the surprise was spoiled and we guessed our presents before Christmas morning. So, she had a secret code list. Everyone was assigned a reindeer name, a different one each year, and those were the names on all the tags. Christmas morning we found out which reindeer we were and which presents were ours."

"Sounds like fun."

"It was. It was great fun," he said, remembering those happy times.

"What happened? Where's your family now? Did they disown you because you became a priest?"

"No, not hardly," he said softly. "They're gone, they've all died."

"All of them?" she asked incredulously.

"All of them."

"Tell me about it."

"I can't. It still hurts too much to talk about it."

She handed him a purple and green striped egg on a yellow ribbon and indicated that he should hang it on the tree by pointing her finger at an empty branch.

"You'll find out that it actually hurts less if you talk about it."

"You sound exactly like me when I'm counseling others. Is that what you're trying to do to me? Counsel me?"

"Do you need counseling, counselor?" she asked with a impudent grin.

And right then he knew he needed her for much more than counseling. He moved back from the tree and turned to go. "I need to get over to the church."

"Why?"

"Because I need to get away from here."

"Why?"

"Missy! Stop It! You know damn well why!" he said over his shoulder as he left the room.

She stared at the empty doorway. He had actually cussed at her! She had a hint of a smile on her face when she turned back to the tree to finish decorating it. He was bothered by her, and he was more than just a *little* bit bothered by her. Well, that was only fair. She was bothered by him. Ex-treme-ly bothered by him. She wanted to find a way to get him to kiss her again. She loved being kissed by him. There was nothing like the feeling she got in the pit of her stomach when he kissed her. The flip-flop and flutterings of a hundred jumping beans making her all nervous and jittery. And even though she wouldn't have thought so, she yearned to feel that deep, achy sensation over and over again.

She finished with the tree, put away the mess, and walked to the door. Just as she reached for the light switch that would turn off the only source of light in the room, the color wheel, she felt a hand close over hers. "Leave it on."

Father Steve's hoarse whisper sent frissons of charged heat scuttling up her back. He turned her and wrapped his hand around her waist drawing her back against his chest. They stood looking at the tree as it rotated into the prisms of light, the colors bouncing off the ceiling and walls. His arms encircled her, and with a contented sigh he rested his chin on top of her head. She placed her hands on his forearms and smiled.

"You came back."

"I couldn't leave you like that."

"Like what?"

"I was angry . . . frustrated."

"Do I frustrate you?" she asked as she turned in his arms.

He looked down into her face and his lips slowly descended to hers. "You know you do," he replied, just before he took her lips with his.

It was a kiss so full of passion, that at first, it scared Missy. His tongue plunged into her mouth seeking to explore her fully, and the roughness of his afternoon shadow abraded her lips as he took full possession her mouth.

The acute awareness of the inevitability of his return coupled with the roughness of his ardor warned him that he had all but lost his sense of control. But right now he didn't care. He simply did not care.

He cupped her face with both hands, pulling her closer and kissing every part of her mouth. He relished the feel of her lips against his and her tongue stroking alongside his as she tentatively explored his mouth. They kissed frantically for several minutes before he eased her back into the room, closed the door, and switched off the light, stopping the color wheel and darkening the room.

"Steve?" she asked timidly.

"What's the matter," he whispered against her throat, "now that you've turned me into a carnally-demented man, are you afraid where it will lead?"

"N-n-no," she stuttered, "just afraid we'll get caught."

"What does it matter?" he asked as he reached for the buttons on her shirt and began unfastening them. As he felt each newly bared section of skin with his fingertips, his lips followed to claim it.

"Are you sure?" she whispered.

"Yes! Dammit! I'm sure!" he said and fumbled with the few remaining buttons. Agitated and confused, he gripped the bottom panels of her shirt and ripped it the rest of the way open. He unsnapped the front clasp of her bra and with his palms flat, smoothed the thin fabric away from her breasts.

"Ahhh. Nice, nice, nice. Your breasts are very, very nice," he said squeezing first one and then the other before bending his head to her chest to suckle on a hard peak.

With his other hand, he reached under her short skirt, hooked the waistband of her panties with his finger and pulled them down to her knees. He walked her toward the back of the room and eased her down onto one of the low wooden tables. He was kissing her chest, rubbing one hand over her furry thatch, and unzipping his zipper all at the same time when he looked down and saw her pale face in the meager shadow of the room. And instantly, he knew he couldn't go through with this. He couldn't take her this way. He was filled with lust, surely more lust than love at this exact moment, when he realized that he was more concerned with fucking her, and possessing her than he was with loving and pleasuring her. He knew that this was wrong, even though he really did believe he could be in love with her. But this, this was lust. This was not thinking of the future, this was hormones, and raging, out of control ones at that.

He removed his hand from her, tucked himself back inside his pants, zipped his zipper, and stood. Then he offered her his hand and helped her up. "Missy, I'm so sorry. I'm not exactly sure what came over me just then. Unbridled, full-blown lust I think. You are absolutely driving me crazy, and I don't know what to do about it."

He walked to the door, and although the room was darkened, she could see the anguish in his handsome face, anguish caused by her and his feelings for her. She was touched by his uncertainty and moved by his loss of control over his emotions. But she really didn't know what to say to this man who had aroused her so fiercely and then deemed that he could not have her.

"I'm sorry," he said again and walked out the door into the brightly lit hallway. He closed the door behind him leaving Missy staring at the thin stream of light coming under the door before forcing herself to sit up and fix her clothing.

Later that evening, Father Steve found himself jogging on the block where Mrs. Hainey lived. It wasn't all that unusual since it was only five blocks away from the church, but it was curious that he'd never chosen this particular route before. As his sneakers slapped the sidewalk in front of Mrs. Hainey's house, he looked up at the light on the top floor. He knew Missy's bedroom was in the attic, and that she was probably at home since dinner had already been served at the rectory. He wondered what she was doing and if she felt as raw about the way they had parted this afternoon as he did. Every part of his body longed for her sweet touch, and his desire to feel himself moving inside her was overwhelming. As every part of his mind screamed that it could never happen, that he could never have her, his heart betrayed him and insisted that he would. Had he known that she was soaking in a bathtub, dreaming of him and reliving his kisses, he might not have been able to run past the house. He might have had to take a detour, a detour that would have sparked the passion they were both feeling at that very moment. The heat from it would catch that old house on fire, and everything would go up in flames, including them.

Chapter Fifteen

When he got back to the rectory there was a message from Frank asking Father Steve to call him. He stared at the number but didn't recognize it. What in the world did Frank want, he thought with disdain. He went up to his room and dialed the number, using the phone on his desk.

When a man answered, he asked for Frank.

"This is Frank."

"Frank?" Father Steve asked. It wasn't the Frank that had murdered his sister and mother. He would recognize that voice anywhere. But this voice he couldn't place.

"Steve! This is Frank. Thanks for calling me back. Listen, I need to talk to you. I'm in my car. Is it all right if I stop over right now?"

Frank, Kelly's Frank. The man she was to marry.
"Yeah. Sure. C'mon over, I'm free."

"Great. I'll be there in about twenty minutes."

He disconnected and stared at the wall where a picture hung that he'd chosen many years ago. It was his favorite—Jesus in the Garden of Gethsemane, tears looking like drops of blood cascading down his face as, his hands were together in prayer.

What could Frank Bowman possibly want with him? He hadn't seen him in years. When Frank arrived twenty-five minutes later, he took him to his downstairs office and closed the door behind them. They took seats across from each other at a small grouping of easy chairs in front of the fireplace.

"I haven't seen you since my father's funeral. What have you been up to?"

"Well Steve, I mean *Father* Steve, that's what I wanted to talk to you about. I'm getting married."

Father Steve closed his eyes and let the words sink in before opening them and saying, "Well Frank, I think that's wonderful." He was dreading what was coming next. Frank had come to ask him to perform the ceremony.

"I have a favor to ask of you."

Here it comes, he thought.

"I would appreciate it if you could recommend someone who will marry us. She's not Catholic, and I haven't been in years, but it's important to my mom that we be married in the church. I'd ask you, but it's pretty important that there be as little connection to Kelly as possible."

"Why?" Now he was hurt because he *hadn't* been asked to marry them.

"Because she looks a lot like Kelly and doesn't know it."

"How is that?"

"How is it that she looks like Kelly, or how is it that she doesn't know that she does?"

"Both."

Frank gave a big sigh then launched into it, "Well, I suppose she looks like Kelly because that's the kind of woman I was looking for when I started dating again. Searching back it seems that I only dated women who had long black hair and laughing blue eyes. She doesn't know any of this because she's very sensitive on the subject of Kelly. She knows how much I loved her, and if she knew how much she favored her, she'd think she was just Kelly's replacement."

"Is she?"

"No. I love Lynne. And I don't want her to spend her life comparing herself to Kelly. I thought you'd understand."

"Oh, believe me, I do. At first, I thought you were going to ask me to perform the ceremony. I was dreading having to tell you that I didn't think that I could. Hearing you say your vows to another woman would be an extremely hard thing for me."

"Yeah. I can see how that would be."

"I'm sure Father Justy or Father Andrews would be more than happy to marry you and Lynne. I'll recommend you. When's the wedding going to be?"

"She wants a fall wedding, I don't really care. I just want to make it down the aisle this time."

"You'll have to take the classes again, but you've got plenty of time for that."

"No problem."

"Frank, do you mind if I ask you a question?"

"No, go ahead."

"Was Kelly a virgin?"

"That's an odd question. Why are you asking?"

"Something was overheard in the dress shop Kelly and Mom were in that day. Kelly said something to Mom about whether she had the right to wear white or not. I thought it might mean something."

Frank looked at Steve but wasn't seeing him. He was remembering a day long ago. He managed a faint smile before saying, "No, she wasn't. Blame it on the Sydney Lutz Drive-In." His smile turned into a frown. "I'm probably the only man alive who can't stand to watch the movie *Bull Durham.* It's not a wonderful memory anymore."

"Thanks, now I won't be able to either," Father Steve said.

They both stood and hugged and clasped each other on the back.

"You take care."

"You have a nice wedding and a happy life."

At the door Frank turned and looked back at Father Steve. "I am settling. I love Lynne. But I know I'll never love anyone as much as I loved Kelly. Sometimes I think God only gives you one chance at a truly miraculous love. Kelly was mine."

All Father Steve could think of as he closed the rectory door behind Frank was that maybe, if it hadn't been for his name, he'd still have her.

On the slow trudge up the steps to his room he was thinking, *Frank is stronger than I am, he's going on . . . .*

Then later that night in bed, he was confronted with the thought that . . . . *Maybe I should too.*

Two days later, Father Steve asked to speak to the Monseigneur, and they sat together in the Monseigneur's formal office sipping tea and watching the late afternoon sun go behind the church spire.

Father Steve came right to the point. He asked for a sabbatical, a particularly long one—the whole summer break. He figured that right after the final exams were graded, he could post the grades, attend the graduation ceremonies, and then fly to Europe. There was research he could do in Italy, and he knew several parishes that would welcome him as a houseguest. He sketched out the scenario of his inheritance and the decisions entailed with that, and even told the Monseigneur about the completely male and lascivious feelings he was having toward one particular parishioner, and some unsettled feelings he was having about his traumatic past.

"I feel like the male version of the super-soprano, mother superior from *The Sound of Music*," the Monseigneur said.

When Father Steve just looked back at him with a perplexed look, the Monseigneur continued in a droning voice, "Climb every mountain, ford every stream, follow every rainbow, blah, blah, blah . . . until you find your dream."

"Oh," was all Father Steve said.

"I can understand you wanting to hightail it out of here and retreat for a while. It's been a long time since you've taken a vacation, but why so long? Why the whole summer?"

"I just need the time to sort things out."

"Time won't make you fall out of love with her."

"What are you talking about?"

"Kid yourself, but you're not kidding me. I don't know about all the other things on your mind, but I certainly know that Missy is. She's the woman who has your gut in knots."

It both shocked and surprised Father Steve that the Monseigneur knew exactly who he was having both amorous and lascivious feelings toward. And, if anything, he seemed to be more encouraging of those feelings than condescending of them.

"H-h-how?" he stammered, confused and embarrassed to have been caught somehow.

"You wear it on your face. In your impatience and restlessness when she's not around, and then in your immediate transformation and undivided attention when she is."

"I hadn't known it was that obvious."

"It may not be to anyone else, but I recognize the signs. I was in your place once, a long, long time ago."

"What happened?"

"Isn't it obvious?"

"You chose the church."

"It was a lot more complicated than your scenario. She was married."

"Well, that does muff it up a bit, doesn't it."

"Yes, it certainly does." There was quiet for a few moments, then he continued. "I saw your stress, your almost constant state of inattentiveness, your unfocused thoughts. That, coupled with your desire to borrow my book, added up to one thing. You know Steven, your attraction to each other is normal, it's human. What you're going to do about it is the dilemma you're facing now. Am I right?"

"So far, you've been right about everything. Everything except why I borrowed your book. It had nothing to do with her. I'm troubled about a confession."

"Ah. I've been there, too. Maybe you're right in taking yourself away for a while. I'll let you go for a month. That ought to be enough time for you to make the decisions you have to make. I'll arrange for the funds."

"That won't be necessary, I have all the money I'll need. It seems I have three pressing problems to deal with, not the least of which is the inheritance I hadn't even known about. But I might as well save the church's money and use some of my own."

"When it rains it pours . . . "

"Tell me about it," he said as he moved to stand up.

"Just remember . . . "

"What?"

The Monseigneur stood up tall from behind his desk, put one hand on his chest and lifted the other into the air before bellowing out in his deep basso voice, "Climb every mountain, search every stream, follow every rainbow, 'til . . . you . . . find . . . your . . . dream!"

Father Steve smiled back at him with a wry grin. "Now I know why your service has the largest choir—how charitable it is of them to take it upon themselves to try to drown you out and spare the rest of us."

"Watch what you say about my singing, your passport is locked in my safe you know," the Monseigneur said with a feigned look of rejection.

"Sing on, mon Virtuoso, sing on," he said with a wave of his hand. Father Steve chuckled to himself as he closed the door behind him. He should have known he couldn't get anything past the Monseigneur. That man truly had an open conduit to God. It would have been a shame if the Monseigneur had followed his heart in his youth and left the church. Years from now, would someone think the same of him? He doubted it. The Monseigneur was a holy man, you could feel it and see it in his face whenever he preached—Father Steve had no such illusions about himself.

 ⧓

The next day after classes, he asked Missy to stay after so he could talk to her about his leaving. She thought he was going to answer a question she had e-mailed him about his comments on her term paper. After the class had disbursed, he walked around the front of his desk and sat on the end of it. She had come up from her seat and sat in the row directly in front of him.

As he gently swung his foot back and forth, he looked down at his not-so-shiny loafer. "Missy, I'm going away for a while."

"Away? Away where?"

"Europe. For the first part of the summer."

"Ohhh. Europe. Take me with you! Please, please."

"That would defeat the whole reason for me leaving. I'm going away to do some thinking—some thinking alone. I need time to try to pull my thoughts together."

"I told you that you needed to talk to somebody."

"True, true," he said with a slight smile, recalling their conversation of a few days ago. "But what I need most right now, is some time away. This Sunday is Easter Sunday. After that we'll have less than a month left of classes, and then I can line up my problems and deal with them one at a time."

"I'm a problem, huh?"

"You are by far, my best problem, but a problem nevertheless. I can't be around you right now. You make it very hard for me to keep my vow of celibacy. One day, priests may be allowed to marry, but I don't see that in the near future. And if I'm going to remain a priest, I have to remain celibate. And you, my dear, are making that unbearably hard for me. Just being around you makes me want you."

"Celibate." She said the word like it was the worst kind of cancer, and he'd just told her he had it.

"Yes, celibate. Celibate means not letting the response take over. Not letting things come to fruition. Abstaining from deriving the ultimate sexual pleasure of release."

"I know what celibate means," she said impatiently. "So you've been celibate for what, eight years now?"

"About that. Until just recently, as you may recall."

She flashed a wry grin, "How do you manage to stay celibate when you're so . . . so virile?"

"I don't let myself dwell on it, I force myself to think of other things. I play basketball. It hasn't really been that much of a problem for me up until now."

"And that's all my fault."

"I wouldn't say 'fault.' "

"Well, what would you say then?"

"It's something that just happened. I know I have always initiated things with us, but you've been more than receptive, more like eager and wanton—which would delight most men. If we cool it and separate for a while, it'll probably all blow over, and when I come back I probably won't even notice that you're beautiful, and bubbly, and full of life, and that you have such wonderfully kissable lips and all those soft, sexy places my fingers itch to touch."

His words melted her and she knew that the only reason he didn't lean over and whisper them to her, was because there were hundreds of coeds walking just outside the open door in full view.

"So, what am I supposed to do? I hope you don't think I'm just going to wait around pining for you to come back, 'cause I have plans, you know. Lots of plans." She had no plans, and they both knew it.

"No, I'm not thinking that at all. I'm thinking that you're going to keep working at the rectory so you can earn your fall tuition, and that you're going to take two summer classes that I've already arranged for you to take, gratis. And that you're going to start dating some of the guys that I know are asking you out on a daily basis."

"Well, what if I don't want to?"

He stood up and reached for his briefcase. "Then don't."

"That's it then? You're going away and I'm stuck here?"

"Yup." He flung his sports coat over his shoulder, picked up his briefcase and headed for the door.

"What are the summer classes?"

He called over his shoulder as he went out the door, "Advanced Strategies of Chess and Introduction to Italian Cooking."

"Italian Cooking?" she called out after him. "Why *Italian* Cooking?"

"So we'll have something to talk about when I get back. I'm going to Italy."

When I get back. Those were the only words she heard. *When I get back.* We'll talk when I get back. That's what he'd said, right?

Chapter Sixteen

The next few weeks were a flutter of activity as spring made its appearance on campus for the last days of classes and final exams. Missy found herself practically falling asleep in class, exhausted from all the late-night studying. After finishing her dinner and kitchen duties at the rectory, she would drag herself home to the Widow Hainey's and force herself to study hour after hour until it seemed, when she finally fell into bed, her bones melted right into the linens. On top of everything, the yellow pollen covering every horizontal surface was awakening her latent allergies and wearing her down even more. She struggled just to make it to her first morning class on time.

She'd hardly had a glimpse of Father Steve, as he was busy tutoring students, preparing exams, and coaching the church softball team. On weekends, her afternoons and evenings were spent sitting on the hard steel bleachers with an open book in her hand, studying, just so she could get a glimpse of him as he shagged balls and fielded grounders. Gad, he looked good in gym shorts.

He noticed her in the stands watching him, and a few times he came by to look at what she was reading, or to annoy her by asking if she knew the score. She never did. She wasn't there to watch the game and he knew it.

The week of finals was grueling, but she didn't want it to be over with, because it meant that he would be leaving just that much sooner. And she really, really didn't want him to go. She would miss him terribly, and he was right; she *would* pine for him until the day he got back.

The afternoon the grades were posted was as emotional a day as she'd ever seen on the campus. Those little computer-generated blips next to the names decided futures, and even as confident as she was of her grades, she found herself nervous right along with the rest of the students. Finally, she made her way up to the board and found her name on each separate class sheet. 'A . . . A . . . A . . . A . . . A . . . B.'

B! He gave her a B! She quickly spun on her heel and marched to his classroom. He wasn't there, so she retraced her steps back to the commons and asked around for his whereabouts. Finally the Admin office told her that he'd checked out. She raced over to the rectory and ran into the main hall—he wasn't there either. Boldly, she stomped up the stairs and faced the closed door to his room. Without even knocking, she turned the handle and pushed it open. He was just coming out of his bathroom, towel drying his hair, and wearing only a white and blue striped towel knotted at his waist. He looked incredible, but right now, she didn't care. She plain didn't care.

"You gave me a B! There is no way I didn't

deserve an 'A!' "

"Close the door," he said calmly, almost as if he had been expecting her.

She turned back to the door and slammed it. He winced at the sound.

"I said close it, not slam it!"

"What difference does it make? It's shut! Now what about my grade?"

He walked to his desk and picked up a white sheet of paper. Scanning it, he said, "What about it? Not many people come to me complaining about getting an 'A.' "

She grabbed the paper out of his hand and found the line that had her name on it. There it was, typed right next to her name: 'A.'

"I don't understand, the sheet posted in the commons . . . I could have sworn it had a 'B' for my grade," she said as she stared at the paper.

"Did you really think I'd be unfair to you," he asked as he stepped closer to her.

"No, I never worried about the grade you'd give me. That's why I was so shocked when I saw it was a 'B.' "

"Seems an apology is due, don't you think?" His voice had lowered, it was sexy and it was implying something—something she wasn't sure she was hearing.

"I . . . I guess I was wrong, but I could have sworn that I read it right. I'm sorry."

"Not good enough," he said and took another step closer. They were touching now, his towel pressed against the hem of her skirt. She could feel the dampness of it against her thighs.

"What do you mean?" she stammered as she

tried to back away from him.

"I mean, you're going to have to do a lot more than say 'I'm sorry,' " He reached down with one hand and whipped his towel off, and suddenly her throat constricted and her mouth went dry.

She licked her lips as she looked up at him. His penetrating gaze looking down was fierce, but the way his damp hair was tousled around his head softened his overall appearance. She wasn't as afraid of him as she probably should have been. She reached up with both hands to smooth his damp curls back from his forehead, never lifting her eyes from his smoldering gaze. Then his eyes fell to her lips, and he bent his head and kissed her. She felt the towel in his hand drop to the floor. Then she felt his arms go around her pulling her close. Her arms had fallen to his shoulders after tangling in the hair at his temples, and now they luxuriated in the feel of his broad shoulders and back as she returned his kiss.

The groan that escaped his lips—as he ended one kiss and began another—lit a fire in her belly, and all she wanted was for this man to lay her on his bed and make her his.

He moved his lips over hers, his tongue darting behind her teeth and lapping at her silky, moist cavity. Every place his tongue stroked, she felt a heated, matching response, and soon she was as frenzied as he was with giving and taking passionate kisses.

Her hands stole down from his shoulders to his chest, and she moaned from the sensation of finding warm, furred skin smoothed over taut muscles. She finally was able to feel the chest she had glimpsed under those loose tank tops he wore when she'd seen him jogging or shooting hoops. It wasn't wet with sweat now, but the thick hairs were still damp from his shower. She let her hands roam with relish over the hard planes of his pecs. He was holding her too close for her to run her hands down the front of him, but she could run her opened palms along the sides of his chest, and graze his ribs with her fingernails.

When her roving fingertips found and outlined the tight, hard bud of a nipple, he gasped. She reveled in the harsh male sound of it, and it was then that she realized she possessed the feminine allure to give him the ultimate sexual release that he had spoken of, the pleasure he had denied himself for so long. If she could bring him to his knees, so to speak, he'd have to come back to her. And before he left tomorrow, she would have to show him how happy she could make him, how well she could pleasure him. She would give him something to think about during those solitary hours in Italy, something he would never forget.

She waited until he had ended a kiss, then softly pressed kisses along his freshly-shaven jaw to his throat. She kissed him and licked him, inhaling deeply his skin's scent. Even newly bathed, he smelled citrusy, and she realized that he must have used cologne after shaving. She trailed a long line of kisses to his chest, and as she moved her hands lower, her mouth followed. He moved his hands to her hips, and held her loosely, allowing her the freedom to cover his chest with light kisses and sweet tongue-lashings. When her lips found his flat nipple with the hardened bud in the center, she mercilessly sucked it into her mouth. His long, low, "Aaaaarghhh," encouraged her, and she moved her hands lower. She ran a flattened palm over his abdomen, enjoying the feel of his warm skin covered with crisp curling hairs, until she felt something nudge the side of her hand. She knew it was his manhood, rising up to meet her caresses, and she grasped it, sending him to his knees.

She followed him to the carpet, and as if she'd done this all her life, she took him into her mouth. His hands went to her shoulders. He tried halfheartedly to pry her away, but she was suddenly of one mind and saw this as a way to secure him to her. In the way that women had used for centuries, she bargained for his love by lavishing his body with her mouth. She took him as deeply into her as she could, mindful not to choke or nip him with her teeth.

The books she had read had not been wrong; there was nowhere near enough room in her mouth to take all of him in. While her hands joined her mouth, smoothing his skin up and down, her tongue licked the sides and the tip of his pulsing shaft. He was almost sobbing now as his hands gripped her hair, urging her closer. And before she knew what to expect, he came, christening her mouth with his climax.

The human sexuality books she had researched had all been vague and ambivalent about what to do with the warm fluid that spurted into her mouth, but she knew that the courtesans of years past as well as today's hardened women of the streets, relished the reward. So, not wanting to be found lacking, she swallowed. The vile consistency as well as the extreme saltiness caused her to shiver and gag, but she was careful not to let him know that the taste of his essence reviled her.

He collapsed onto the floor in a crumpled heap, pulling her against his chest and holding her in his arms. He stroked her neck and face trying to quell his shaking and trembling body.

"Definitely an 'A,'" he whispered into her ear, his lips softly caressing her hair. "This extra credit project of yours is the most creative project I've ever had a student turn in."

She looked up at him and smiled softly, "I didn't need any extra credit to get my 'A.'"

"No, you didn't," he readily agreed as his hands made large circles on her back.

They were silent for a few moments, then he said, "You're trying to make it impossible for me to leave, aren't you?"

"Did it work?"

"No. I still have to go. But I fear the reunion when I get back a month from now. This isn't something I will easily forget."

"Mission accomplished then," she said and she tucked her head under his arm.

"That was all book learnin' huh?" he asked leaning over her, his head propped on his hand to look down at her.

"You'd be surprised what's in the university library and on the Internet."

"I already know what a good researcher you are. Now I know how well you can apply practical aspects from the written word. You were incredible."

"I'm rather pleased with the results myself," she said with a huge grin.

He rumpled her hair even more than it was already, and leaned over to kiss her. "I imagine everyone is wondering what you've been doing in my room for so long, especially since they know I'm up here. It didn't help that you announced your presence by slamming the door."

"I was really angry about my grade."

"I know. I knew you would be."

She pushed away from him and sat up. "What? What do you mean you knew I would be?"

Sheepishly, he ducked his head then lifted it abruptly to face the music. "I purposefully hung that dummied sheet in the commons knowing that it would spur you to find me. I wanted to see you alone one more time before I left. I knew you'd find me. I just didn't know that you'd barge right in on me without even knocking."

"You wanted to say good bye?"

"Something like that. I never dreamed this would happen," he said as he indicated his naked body with his outstretched hand.

"Disappointed?"

"Not in a million years," he said and drew her close for a kiss. It was a claiming kiss, a kiss that meant: *I don't know what this is all about yet, but wait for me, and we'll figure it out together.*

He stood up and gently pulled her up with him, reached for his towel and wrapped it around himself. "Go downstairs to my office and wait for me while I get dressed. I'll just be a few minutes. I want to set up an e-mail account for you so we can keep in touch while I'm in Italy."

"It won't do any good. I don't have a computer to access it."

"You can use the one in the university library, or when you're here, you can use the one in my office. I'll make sure everyone knows that it's okay for you to use it."

He came to her and smoothed her tousled curls with his fingers, marveling at the soft, baby fine spirals. He bent to take her lips lightly with his. Before their lips touched, he whispered, "A straight 'A' student, a good cook, great athlete, gives exceptional blow jobs, you're gonna make someone a wonderful wife. Shame you're just a middlin' chess player."

She allowed him to kiss her before she turned to the door, opened it and retorted, "That's what you think, you've just been checkmated and you don't even know it."

He stroked his jaw as he walked to the bathroom. Oh, he knew it all right.

When he went for his evening jog, it was a bit later than usual; he'd had a lot of loose ends to see to before leaving in the morning. Again, he took the path less taken, namely the one in front of the Widow Hainey's. He stopped in front of the house, his hands on his hips trying to catch his breath—and a glimpse of her.

He saw the light on the top floor blazing bright and wondered what Missy was reading. Then he noticed that Mrs. Hainey's car was not in the driveway, and he vaguely recalled a parishioner saying that she was going to Ohio to visit her sister.

The temptation was too great. He straightened, wiped the sweat from his face with his shirtfront, and walked up the front walkway to the porch steps. After deliberating, berating himself, and praying, he rang the bell. Moments later he heard someone running down the stairs. Missy's face appeared in the glass side panel. She smiled up at him and unlocked the door before opening it wide and welcoming him in.

This was a big mistake, he thought, as he

stepped into the foyer. But apparently she did not think so as she grabbed his hand and led him back toward the parlor.

"Well, isn't this a surprise."

"I was jogging and just wanted to see if you might be at the window or something. Then I noticed Mrs. Haineys' car was gone and I remembered . . ."

"That she's away?"

"Yes, that she's away."

"As in not here," Missy added.

"Precisely." Father Steve pulled her into his arms and against his chest.

"I want you," he whispered, kissing her jaw line and French kissing her ear.

"Then you're in luck, for today, I can be yours for a very reasonable price."

"Yeah, and what's that?" he asked in a gruff voice as he bent her over his arm and splayed the panels on her bathrobe open. She was warm and her skin rosy as if she'd just come from her bath. He recognized the nightgown he had given her under it. He ran a flat palm down between her breasts, stopping with his hand covering her belly.

"A kiss, the payment I would demand is a kiss. World class, mind you."

"I'll give you world class," he breathed against her neck, lifting her and carrying her into the parlor. He placed her on the edge of a large upholstered chair then gently pushed her back until her head was on the seat, and her feet were on the floor in front of her. He ran his hands up her thighs taking both bathrobe and nightgown with them, settling the material over her hips. Her dark curls were still damp from her bath. His hands parted her robe and pushed her nightgown up over her breasts.

"It's been so long since I've seen a woman in all her glory. I had forgotten how marvelous God's handiwork is." His hand strayed to her curls, and he ran his fingers through them as he studied her.

With a hand on each knee he spread her thighs wide and knelt reverently between them. She felt his hands caress up her inner thighs, wrap around her hips, shift her bottom high, and lift her to his mouth.

Soft kisses and sweet lashings of his exploring tongue had her closing her eyes against the intense pleasure. Never had she imagined that anything could feel so good, so right . . . and so ooohhh . . . his tongue, mating with her, slid into every crevice and claimed her. His fingers, spreading her wide, held her open while his thumb roamed over her slickness and entered her. When his mouth clamped onto her and suckled the area at the top of her slit, her legs shook and she convulsed against his greedy mouth. Over and over again he brought her to the peak and then sent her into a deep abyss where the back of her eyes became a backdrop for a myriad of rainbow prisms. The last time, she felt and heard him moan against her. His hands on her hips, securing her to his mouth, he trembled, and she felt him relax his hold. She had asked for a world-class kiss and she got it; she just hadn't specified where.

He hadn't realized how erotic pleasuring her would be, or that watching her climax would lead to his own. He was now insensate, and humbled by this gift God had devised for a man and a woman to share.

She looked between her legs, which somehow ended up on his shoulders, and saw his dark head move back and forth as he kissed her thighs all the way down to her knees. Gripping one foot, he straightened her leg and kissed down to the ankle before placing it on the floor. The other leg was next.

He stood looking down at her and swore.

"Are you angry?" she asked as she covered herself and scooted up on the seat.

"Of course I'm angry. This should not have happened. Look at you, I ravished you, and I couldn't stop. I have a jock strap that can't go in the laundry tomorrow, and now I don't want to leave you, I want to take you to bed, love you some more, and sleep with you in my arms."

"So why don't you?"

"Well for one thing my flight leaves at 6:45 in the morning, and I haven't packed yet. For the other, it would not do either of us any good for one of your neighbors to see me leave in the middle of the night."

She leaned up, drew him down and kissed him. "So go then—go think about me. Think about us. Think about what you want from me."

"I already know what I want from you."

"And what's that?"

He slid his hand between the folds of her bathrobe and caressed her silky curls, "More of this, all of this, every bit of this. Wait for me."

With that, he removed his hand and stood, "I need to use your bathroom before I leave. Don't see me out, I can't take much more of saying goodbye to you."

Chapter Seventeen

Via E-mail

Father Steve

Florence is wonderful. I'll never get enough of this place. Yesterday I drove around the countryside taking pictures. I can't wait to show them to you. One day you must come here. I hope you aren't missing any of those cooking classes, because I'm getting pretty addicted to the cuisine. I've probably gained five pounds from all the wonderful pasta dishes. I hope all is well with you. F.S.

Missy

I learned to make Cannelloni yesterday. Today it's Pasta Fagioli and the ladyfingers to begin making a Tiramisu. Pretty good stuff, this Italian food. I make a great tomato basil sauce if do I say so myself. Bring back some canned tomatoes—my teacher says there's nothing like the tomatoes grown in Italy. I seem to be Chef Marchinio's pet student. He even let me use his very own, very expensive, imported mandolin. I think I can get an 'A' in this class with my eyes closed. Going to make it to the Vatican and get an audience with you-know-who? M.R.

Father Steve

You'd better not be earning that 'A' the way you tried to earn one with me! I'm not sure I like the idea of you being anybody's pet—make sure you let him know about the big bruiser you've got for a 'father,' and it wouldn't hurt any to let him know that he speaks Guido's language—fluently. The Pope says I can come see him if I want to, but the only day he's available is the same day Sophia Loren wants to see me, so I told him I'd have to hook up with him some other time. Just joking of course, sadly, neither one even knows I'm here. Can't wait to try your gourmet homework. I'll try to remember about the tomatoes. And, please, please, keep your eyes open, especially when you're using the mandolin. I like every one of your fingers. F.S.

Missy

What an exciting week we've had here. Frank, the handyman got arrested. I'm not exactly sure what for yet, something about a summons he didn't reply to. They took him in and got a subpoena for a DNA sample, but it's going to be a few weeks before they figure out if the charges are going to stick. So I've been running around trying to raise his bail money. We finally raised the bail last night. It took three bake sales, two car washes, a yard sale, a bingo rally, and a fairly large donation from the parishioners. But we finally did it! I'm really proud of myself; I would have felt badly if he'd had to spend any more time in jail. He seems like such a nice guy. Don't fill up on too many cannolis, everyone at the rectory says mine are to die for. Hope you don't mind . . . but Chef Marchinio has an extra credit project for me. Get your mind out of the gutter. He wants me to help cater a party with him, AND he's going to pay me! Does that mean I'm a professional cook now? I dropped out of the chess class, no one else ever showed up, and I think the professor teaching the class was bored with watching me set up the whole game just so I could castle. I love that move! M.R.

Father Steve

Missy, I was very distressed to hear about Frank, but not for the reason you think. I dearly wish that you hadn't arranged for his bail. Do not ask me any questions about this; just do EXACTLY as I say. Make sure that Frank knows that you're not a virgin (I know that you will be lying, but I don't care—just do it!!!) and find a way to let him know that you've slept around a lot and that because of it, you now have herpes, genital warts and Chlamydia. Missy, I mean this! Do it and do it as soon as you can. I'm glad the cooking class is going so well. I'll be home in two weeks to try out the haute cuisine, and I'll remember to go for your rooks the next time we play. F.S.

Missy

I did what you said, but I'm sure Frank thinks it was a little weird that I spouted off about my smarmy sex life when I ran into him while he was plunging a toilet. Are you going to tell me what this is all about? How was Sophia? Are you going to make it to Modena? If so, Chef says they have the best balsamic vinegar . . . also, if customs lets you bring it in, we could use some fresh pancetta. It is very hot here, the guys aren't even playing round ball. Gotta go, the Monseigneur just dropped a whole jar of pickles on the kitchen floor. He said something in Latin, and it sounded dirty somehow. Do you guys cuss in Latin so we won't know that you're cussing? M.R.

Father Steve

As long as Frank knows you're not virginal, I don't care where it was or how it was that you told him, as long as you were believable. You were, weren't you? And no, I'm not going to tell you what it's all about, just forget about it now. I absolve you of the sin of lying. Say a Hail Mary for your penance. Seems like you want me to do some grocery shopping before I head back. I'll get what I can. Do I have a surprise for you! Something I found in a little out of the way shop in Assisi. I think you'll like it. Bet you had a dickens of a time getting that kitchen floor clean. I just know the very first time I pad around in there with bare feet that I'll find a spot you missed and my feet will stick. I hate that. Are you accusing the holy men of the church of swearing? I can't believe that you would suggest such a thing! F.S.

Missy

Steve, a Father Bryant has been calling for you. He says it's urgent, for you to call him as soon as you get back. I didn't tell him I was in contact with you, in case you didn't want to talk to him. But he sounded pretty upset. I'm helping teach a summer Catechism class, so I'm up to my ears in little lost sheep. Talk to you later. M.R.

He sat for a few minutes thinking but had such a bad feeling about Missy's e-mail that he reopened his laptop and found Father Bryant's number. Ten minutes later, he was on the phone talking to him.

"So you don't think Frank's getting any better?"

"Not at all. In fact, he's getting worse. Since his arrest, he's been a different man. This case is way over my head. I'm talking to you about it because you referred him, and he told me that you already knew his history. Good God, I can only imagine how you're dealing with all this . . . your own sister and mother. . ., although I'm sure he isn't aware of all that. By the Saints, I just don't know what to do."

"My God, Jeb . . . you're the expert! I don't know what to tell you."

"Steve, we gotta get him more help."

"I don't see how. You know the confidentiality matters as well as I do. Heck, you have two confidences you have to worry about—clinical *and* clerical."

"Yeah, I know. That's why I had to talk to you."

"You had to talk to me because I'm the only one you *can* talk to."

"Yeah," he said with a big sigh.

"I'll talk to him when I get back. Maybe you can do some research and see who is experienced in this kind of thing, someone I can get him to go to."

"Okay."

"I'll call you when I get back."

"Don't take too long."

"Why?"

"Because I think he's looking for another victim."

The blood in Father Steve's veins turned ice cold, and a tremor of panic surged through him.

"How long do we have?"

"I don't know."

"I'll get the next flight back."

"Thanks."

Father Steve dropped the phone in its cradle and stared at the vista out the window of the little villa he was staying in. He was visiting a priest in a remote hamlet about fifty miles from the nearest city. This time his eyes didn't see the majestic mountains rising up to meet the sky, or the goats and the children playing on the green velvet hillside. What they did see were trails of blood and dull, vacant eyes staring back at him, Kelly's lifeless eyes. Instantly, he thought of Missy. Missy with her twinkling, laughing eyes. Missy with her sweet sensuous mouth. Missy with her bouncing, exuberant energy. Missy with her childlike, virginal innocence.

He had to get back. He had to get back and make sure she was safe. He had to make sure Frank didn't find out that she was still a virgin.

He picked up the phone and tried to call her at the church. They hadn't seen her since she had left after teaching her Catechism class. Someone thought she would be back to fix dinner, but someone else said she had left a crock pot cooking and that she wouldn't be back. He left her a message to e-mail him right away.

For the next four hours, he alternately checked his e-mail and called the airlines to see if they had been able to find him a flight. At seven o'clock that night the airlines finally called and said they could get him on a flight to the States if he could get there in two hours. He was roughly two hours away from the airport, but he told them that he would be there.

He hurriedly grabbed his suitcase and ran for the only car in the little burg. The teenaged son of the local wine master owned it. The car was a sporty Italian job that looked like it could fly. He whipped out the Italian equivalent of two hundred dollars and told him it was his if he could get him to the airport in less than two hours. The boy grabbed the money, popped open the trunk to load the suitcase and jumped into the driver's seat. One hour and forty-six minutes later he stood on the tarmac waiting for them to push the stairs back up to the plane. He had made it. He didn't know if his heart would ever be the same, but he'd made it.

Chapter Eighteen

Missy sat in front of the computer in an alcove at the university library, randomly hitting the check mail icon as she worked on the rectory grocery list propped on a book in her lap. She was waiting for Father Steve's reply. She had finally read his early morning message and was doing as he instructed, only he wasn't responding. She looked at her watch, the library would be closing soon—she'd give him five more minutes. She hit the button again and waited for the almost-instantaneous, big red X to cross over the "You've got new mail" message. Then she focused on her shopping list again. Maybe the priests would like a nice taco casserole, she thought as she tapped her pencil against her lips, something to spice things up a bit.

Since Father Steve had left, her days were nothing if not boring, and her mundane chores were starting to grate on her. She hit the key once more, and after getting the expected negative answer, she moved her hand to the mouse to start the shut down procedure. A finger tapping her on the shoulder distracted her, and she turned to see one of the young Jesuits staring down at her.

"Father Steve just called the rectory using an airfone. He's got everybody running around looking for you. He wants you to know that he's on his way back. He'll probably get here sometime in the middle of the night. He said to tell you to stay at the rectory in your old room until he gets here."

"Why?"

"I have no idea. But he was pretty insistent that someone find you right away and make sure you did as he asked."

"Okay, sure. No problem. I was planning on going to the grocery store to pick up a few things and bring them back there anyway. By the way, are you out of barbecued Fritos yet? Do I need to put them on the grocery list?"

"Yeah, that would be great. A big bag this time," he grinned.

"You're on," she said as she stood up and gathered her things together, "I'll get the biggest bag they've got and some chocolate Yahoos, too."

"You're too good to me. When I get to be Pope, I'll commend you for sainthood."

She gave him a big smile and scooted out of her seat, not remembering that behind the now-blank screen, she was still on line, signed on with her password to the server.

A few minutes later, Frank took her newly vacated seat. His arm bumped the keyboard as he sat down in front of the computer that had put itself to sleep. The screen flashed back to life and a low mechanical voice prompted, "No new mail," repeating the last command that hadn't been acknowledged.

Frank had been waiting for an opportunity to use the library's computer all day. He was upset about having been arrested a few days ago, and now he just had to check the State's on-line child molester registry to see if he was listed. That was the only way they could have traced him all the way from Oregon so quickly, he reasoned. He was probably in the system, a local kid must have been groped somewhere nearby, and he'd been pulled in for questioning. Man, if this was a sampling of how it was going to be for him, he'd have to hurt somebody. This was bullshit!

He looked at the page that came up on the screen. He'd learned a little computer savvy in prison and recognized the program someone had left active.

What the hell, he thought and punched the check mail button. *No new mail.* He felt like eavesdropping, taking a vicarious peek at someone else's life, so he moved the mouse and clicked on the 'in' section of the mailbox. Lots of letters, all from the same sender: "RoundballChampion@aol.org." In the subject box one column over, Father Steve was listed as the subject for each missive.

Well, this was interesting. He didn't know who Father Steve was writing to, but apparently he was writing quite often. He highlighted the bottom line and double clicked to open the last e-mail.

What he read there caused his eyes to bulge . . .

Father Steve

As long as Frank knows you're not virginal, I don't care where it was or how it was that you told him, as long as you were believable. You were, weren't you? And no, I'm not going to tell you what it's all about, just forget about it now. I absolve you of the sin of lying. Say a Hail Mary for your penance . . .

Whoa! What the hell was this? He tapped the keys bringing forward each preceding incoming letter.

. . . Missy, I was very distressed to hear about Frank, but not for the reason you think. I dearly wish that you hadn't arranged for his bail. Do not ask me any questions about this; just do EXACTLY as I say. Make sure that Frank knows that you're not a virgin. (I know that you will be lying, but I don't care—just do it!!!) Find a way to let him know that you've slept around a lot and that because of it, you now have herpes, genital warts and Chlamydia. Missy, I mean this! Do it and do it as soon as you can. I'm glad the cooking class is going so well. I'll be home in two weeks to try out the haute cuisine and I'll remember to go for your rooks the next time we play. F.S.

Then:

You'd better not be earning that 'A' the way you tried to earn one with me . . .

Followed by the e-mail listed at the top of the page:

Florence is wonderful, I'll never get enough of this place . . .

His fingers flew back to the mailbox selection and hit the 'out' box, starting with the last message sent:

Steve, a Father Bryant has been calling for you. He says it's urgent, for you to call him as soon as you get back. I didn't tell him I was in contact with you in case you didn't want to talk to him. But he sounded pretty upset. I'm helping teach a summer Catechism class, so I'm up to my ears in little lost sheep. Talk to you later. M.R.

His eyes went wide with shock and anger. Frank continued reading until he had read every e-mail Father Steve and *Missy* had sent each other. *Missy. Missy* who had helped bail him out. *Missy*, who had lied to him that day he'd been plunging some overindulged priest's shit out of the plumbing system. *Missy*, who had convinced him she wasn't his virgin, even though his body's attraction had hinted that she was the very first time he'd even seen her. *Missy!*
He was furious! They had been playing him. First Father Steve by forcing her to lie to him, then by Missy herself, denying him what was rightfully his by pretending to be something she wasn't. She was HIS goddamn it! She was his virgin! And somehow, he'd known it all along, and these two had schemed to keep him from her! That damned filthy priest wanted her for himself. He just knew it! Father Steve wanted HIS virgin, the one that had been promised to HIM, and look what he'd done to keep her from him. He was a bigger sinner than all the rest. He was no better than all those rutting, fuck-happy altar boys! So pious! He was pitiful! Now he'd show him, he'd take her right out from under Father Steve's nose. Her virgin membranes would tear to his manhood, and she would exalt in him. Just as he'd been promised so long ago.
He slammed his fist down on the keyboard, obliterating everything on the screen and making it go dark, sending all the data back to the folder from whence it had come before crashing. He shoved himself out of the chair, sending it banging against the desk behind him. The startled librarian looked over at him

with censure in her eyes, but he was too angry to even notice. He stomped out of the library and made his way to the darkened church. Prayer. Powerful prayer was what he needed before he took her in the mating ritual. The ritual that would make her his for all eternity.

The ritual that was burned into his teenaged memory. Once a week, when his aunt was at midnight mass, he would lie in his bed and stare at the ceiling, tears streaming down his cheeks. Through the thin walls in the old row house he heard his uncle say, "You're mine, you're mine," over and over again as the headboard repeatedly hit the wall while his uncle fucked his mother. Now that his brother's widow was under his roof he had the woman he had always desired, the woman he had first kissed, the woman who had repeatedly stirred his loins but always left him wanting. And each night, after he had taken her with force and withdrew at his leisure, he would slap her face and hiss, "You should have been my virgin! You should never have left me for him! Now you're just my whore. I own you." It had been no secret that his father had wooed her away from his older brother the day after his brother had proposed. It was a rejection that had blighted the family and kept the brothers estranged for so many years. When his father had died in an accident, they'd had no money and no place to live, and no idea of the lust his uncle had harbored for his mother throughout the years. Until his mother died, his uncle had sated his lust every Saturday night while his wife was at church. And Frank had been forced to listen as his uncle chanted, "You're mine, you're mine. My virgin, my virgin," to the pounding of the headboard. It had eventually become a mantra he could not get out of his head.

Chapter Nineteen

This had been the longest flight of his life, Father Steve thought as he hailed a cab in front of the terminal. All the way across the Atlantic his thoughts had jumbled and tumbled one over the other as his stomach clenched and his heart raced. He thought about many things, although one thought had challenged all the others: Repentance—Latin for change of heart. Well, he'd certainly had a change of heart. He now knew that he loved Missy, loved her enough to go against his vows to protect her from a demonic killer. And he loved her enough to change everything, not just his heart. But had Frank truly repented, had *his* heart changed, or was it still evil and warped? Could the man be truly remorseful? Had he atoned and earnestly decided to give his life to the church in penance for his grievous transgression? If need be, was he ready give himself up and face prison to pay for his sins?

Father Steve just couldn't take the chance, he couldn't trust or forgive, and that was when he realized that there had never been any point in trying. "Vengeance is mine," sayeth the Lord. So is forgiveness. He told himself that forgiveness had never been an option open to him, that it was time for him to stop beating himself over the head because he couldn't. God didn't expect him to forgive Frank for what he had done, he only expected him to show Frank the way to receive his forgiveness from God, if that's what he truly desired.

His heart had changed, and he would take better care of it this time. He wouldn't let it fill up with bitterness and regret. He'd fill it with hope and love and the happiness God had shown him he could have by loving Missy as God had meant for a man to love a woman.

He patted the cherished package that sat as a small lump in his jacket pocket. Yes, he did have the surprise for Missy that he had promised her. And it would be a surprise for the whole congregation too, when the church bells pealed and he and his new bride wended their way from the altar to the long center aisle and down the enormous stone steps of the cathedral.

He urged the cab driver to go faster than the law allowed, then felt guilty as the man stared at his roman collar in the rear view mirror. It felt more foreign than it had ever felt before, and he smiled at the thought that soon he would take it off and never feel the uncomfortable chaff of it against his skin again.

Chapter Twenty

A light tapping on her door woke Missy, and she turned to squint at the small wedge of light behind the silhouette of a man's frame.

"Steve?" she whispered.

"It's Frank, Miss Roberts. I need your help. There's a small child cryin' in one of the chapels. She's askin' for you and says she won't leave 'til you come see her. I don't know what to do, she's real upset and all alone, sobbing her heart out. I can't imagine what's the matter with her."

Missy leapt out of her bed, grabbing for her robe that was twisted into the bed covers. She turned her back to Frank who was still standing in the doorway, as she shoved her arms into the robe. "Who is it?" she asked, "Is it Maddy? She's been having a lot of problems at home."

"Don't know. She's got pretty blonde hair though."

"It's not Maddy then, show me where she is. Why were you in the chapel so late tonight, Frank?"

"I was praying and lost track of the time when I heard these little mewling sounds."

Missy followed him down the dark hallway,

through the connecting door to the church and then to a stairwell on the opposite side at the back of the church. She didn't think she'd ever been in this part of the church before. "I thought you said she was in one of the chapels. Where are we going?"

"She's down here, just a little further."

That was the first time Missy had a hint that maybe something was wrong. She felt a tremor of trepidation travel up her spine and turned to go back through the stairwell door. But he had seen the sudden fear in her eyes. He grabbed her wrist, propelling her away from the steel door and the sanctuary of the sacred chapel.

She screamed, but it was too late, the steel door had closed firmly behind them, and she knew that there wouldn't be anybody on this side of the church at this time of the night to hear her screams.

He cupped his hand over her mouth. "You feel like screaming now, but you won't in a few minutes. You'll be praisin' me and worshipping me, and you'll be mine forever. You'll see. It's gonna be all right."

The wide-eyed terror in her eyes unsettled him for a moment, but then he remembered what he'd been promised. This was the way it was supposed to be, she was supposed to be his. He dragged her down two levels of concrete steps, then pulled her down a long dark hallway. She kicked and arched her body against his hip trying to get away, but he was much stronger than she was, and all she did was make him angrier. There were lights in little cages every twenty feet or so, and she could tell that they were in some kind of basement. When she balked and braced her feet and wouldn't go any further, he picked her up and tossed her over his shoulder. She started screaming again, and he smacked her hard on her bottom.

"I don't like you screaming like that! Cut it out!"

She screamed louder and beat on his back with her fists while kicking at him with her feet. He gripped her legs even tighter while his body deflected the meager assault her fists were making.

"Let me go!" She screamed at the top of her lungs, and using her nails, dug long trenches up his back.

He hollered and threw her down onto the concrete floor, then bent down and slapped her across the face. "Don't do that!" he yelled at her. He kicked open a door, grabbed her under her arms and dragged her backwards into the room. All the while she kicked and pulled against him, and screamed as loud as she could.

When he slammed the door behind them she knew for certain that no one would hear her now. No one would probably ever find her here in this subterranean tunnel. They were in the bowels of the church, somewhere deep below the sanctuary, where all the loud machinery that kept the church running was kept—so low in the building that even the residual humming and hissing of furnaces and pipes wouldn't be heard by a worshipping parishioner upstairs in a chapel. She doubted that the Monseigneur even knew this room existed.

He pushed her toward a rollout bed with a grungy blanket on top. She'd wondered where Frank lived— she knew he was homeless and had even thought about giving him her old VW that was parked on one of the university parking lots. Now, she knew he'd been living here, in this cramped little utility room, and it was pretty certain that no one knew it.

"Remove your night clothes and lay down on that bed," he instructed.

"No! I won't!" she said, moving toward the door.

"You'll do as I say," he hissed and threw her back onto the bed.

He started unbuckling his belt, and her eyes widened in fear. "I don't care what he told you, you're my virgin, not his! And I don't appreciate you lying to me about it!"

She had no idea what he was talking about, but figured she had to find out, if only to stall him. "Frank, I'm not a virgin, I told you that."

"Yeah, you told me that all right. But I found out that it's not true. You're still pure. You're chaste, and you're still waitin' for your altar boy. Well, just so's you don't get the wrong idea, *I'm* your altar boy *not* Father Steve! Much as he'd like you to think so!"

"Altar boy? You're an altar boy?"

"Yeah. I was an altar boy here for years and years. It's not somethin' you outgrow you know. It's like being a priest, just on a smaller scale. It never leaves you though, you're always serving God." He had his belt undone, his zipper down, and his dingy khaki work pants were hanging low on his hips. He pulled his penis out of the opening in his underwear. It was not very impressive, but she was still terrified. Good God, what was she going to do? He was going to rape her! Then a thought came to her. She had no idea if it even had a chance, but she had to try something.

"Don't you think we should pray about this first? I mean it's a really big moment in both our lives."

"Yeah, you're right, it is. Sure, come kneel by me and we'll pray about our consummation together."

"Consummation? What you're getting ready to

do here Frank is called rape."

"Nah, it just seems like that to you now. When it's all over with, you'll exalt in me, you'll be my bride. You'll see. This is God's plan for us." He grabbed her hand and pulled her down beside him.

"Let's pray in the church," she suggested, trying to stand.

"No. *For wherever two or more are gathered in my name there am I in the midst of them, Matthew 18:20.* We are our own church," he said, keeping her from standing with a firm grip on her arm.

They knelt side by side on the cold concrete floor. Her robe had slipped off her shoulder and Frank pulled it down from her back and it fell over her lower legs and feet. She was only in her nightgown now, and she knew that it was practically transparent. It was the one Father Steve had bought her and since she slept in it every night, it was getting pretty worn. She was scared, cold, and didn't know what to do. So she prayed. If this was a God-fearing man, maybe it would truly help. If so, she'd pray and pray and pray. She'd pray until someone rescued her from this madman holding her in the basement of her church. "Our Father, who art in heaven . . ."

Chapter Twenty-one

The door to her room was open and Father Steve peeked inside. "Missy?" There was no answer. "Missy? Are you in here?" He pushed the door all the way open and walked over to the bed. He pressed his palm to the linens in the center. They were still warm. Maybe she was in the bathroom. There was no light under the door, but he knocked anyway. It easily swung open. No one was there.

Panic set in, and he spun around, his eyes frantic as he tried to find her in the semi-darkness.

Then he rousted everyone. He banged on doors then kicked them open, not giving the occupant a chance to sit up in bed and call out. When finally everyone was awake and made aware that he believed Frank had taken Missy, and that he planned on raping her, they all spread out trying to find her.

Father Steve was at his wit's end; they had looked everywhere, and there was no sign of her, but he knew that Frank had her. He felt it. He ran back to her room to see if there was some clue that he had missed. Then he took a deep breath, knelt beside her bed and began to pray, "Our Father, who art in heaven . . . "

Suddenly, he jumped up. He never knew why the word came to him, but it did. *Basement.* Frank had taken Missy to the basement. He knew it. Just as Kelly had been in a basement, that's where Missy was now. He ran down the hall and bumped into the Monseigneur, "Where's the basement?"

"Basement?" the Monseigneur asked, his face blank.

"Boiler room? Where's the furnace, the hot water heaters?"

"Oh! It's on the other side of the chapel, down the stairwell in the back where the storage closet is for the mops and buckets."

Father Steve put his hands on the Monseigneur's shoulders and moved him out of the way. Leaning him back up against a wall, he looked into the old man's face, the expression of helplessness he saw there filled him with sudden inspiration and he whispered. "Pray for Missy, Father. Pray that I'm not too late." He ran through the dark, quiet church heading for the most remote part of the huge edifice.

Chapter Twenty-two

Enough praying already!" Frank stood up and grabbed her elbow. "Get on the bed. It's time."

"I'm not a virgin!" she screamed.

"Yes, you are. I read your e-mails. I know you lied to me. And now I know why," he said menacingly as he walked toward her, his knees pressing against hers, forcing her onto the bed.

"Why?" she asked truly perplexed.

"Because Father Steve told you to, because he knows what I did. He knows I raped a woman and killed her and her mother. He knows about my first virgin and how she was stolen from me."

It all made sense now. All at once, the pieces of the puzzle came together in her mind and she gasped, "You, you raped and killed his sister and his mother!" she accused in a wavering, throaty whisper. The horror was just too much to absorb. "It was you! You! You're the one whose confession caused all his turmoil and self-doubt! He had to go away because of you!" she screamed. In her sudden anger, she drew her knees up to her chest and with all the force she could muster, she kicked him in the chest, sending him sprawling backward to the floor.

She hurriedly got up and jumped over his splayed body and made her way to the door. Just as she grabbed the handle, he caught her ankle and yanked her back. There was spittle around his mouth, and his eyes were gleaming with lust when he stood up. He spun her around and threw her back onto the bed. "I didn't know it was his sister, or his mother, or I sure wouldn't have confessed to him! Do you think I'm an idiot! Now, you're my virgin, and I get to take you! When you come to adore me, you won't care what I did before, it won't matter. Father Steve can't tell what he knows 'cause he's a priest, and after I take you, you won't tell either."

He pulled his semi-erect penis out of his underwear and pumped it a few times with his closed fist. She could see the glistening, swollen red crown of it and it terrified her. He leaned over, forcing her down, and pulled the hem of her nightgown up to her waist. "Ah, my sweet virgin," he said as he parted her thighs and stared down at her womanhood. She lifted a leg to kick against his chest again, but he was ready for it this time and grabbed her ankle. "Now, now, that's not the way to exalt in me. You'll know better in just a few minutes." His other hand grabbed her other leg, and he pulled her to the edge of the bed. She screamed with all her might while her hands clawed at his face.

Suddenly, the door burst open and Father Steve grabbed the back of Frank's low-slung pants, pulling him off balance. He fell to the floor and Father Steve saw Missy naked and splayed on the edge of the bed. The powerful emotions that filled him were no longer to be denied. All the anger and pain he'd hidden deep inside erupted. He jumped onto Frank who was now struggling to get back on his feet. Father Steve began pummeling him. His fists made one solid connection after another, hitting Frank's face so hard that the bones gave way as they yielded to each brutal strike. Over and over he laid into him, not holding back. And with each succeeding forceful blow, Frank's moans and grunts became fewer and fewer. When Missy saw that Frank was no longer capable of defending himself, that he, in fact, was not even conscious anymore, she jumped off the bed and tried to pull Steve away. But she was unable to; he was almost demonic in his quest to punch the last breath out of the man.

A group of young Jesuits made their way down the stairwell and into the small room and even they were unable to separate Steve from Frank. But finally, Steve froze, shook his head as if coming out of a trance and dropped Frank to the floor. He was covered with Frank's blood; his fists, his shirt, his pants, even his shoes had Frank's blood on them. Missy stood beside him letting him support himself on her as he caught his breath, heedless of the blood staining her thin nightgown and smearing her arms.

While the others lifted Frank and carried him out into the hallway where he would wait for an ambulance, Steve leaned down and placed a kiss behind Missy's ear. "Did he hurt you?" he asked. They both knew what he meant.

"No. You have a very good sense of timing, thank God."

"I don't think so," he said as he nuzzled her neck, his panting evidence of his exhaustion, "if I'd timed this right you wouldn't even have been in the running for Frank's virgin hunt. I'd have taken that honor away from you a long time ago."

She smiled up at him and murmured, "Well, it's

not too late."

"Lady, as soon as I'm able, we'll to take care of that little problem once and for all."

She looked up into his eyes with a questioning look on her face, "Really?"

"Really," he said as he bent and took her mouth with his, heedless of everyone around gaping at them. He groaned in pain as he bent to pick up her robe. "Here, put this on. I don't think I have another fight for your honor in me tonight."

When she had slipped her robe on, he took her hand in his and led the curious procession up the stairs and back to the rectory. Two of the priests remained with Frank until the E.M.T.s took him to the hospital.

After ascertaining that Missy was all right, the Monseigneur sent everyone back to bed and talked to the police. He arranged for them to come in the morning to get statements. It was four a.m., Frank was on his way to the hospital; Missy, who had declined any medical treatment, her cuts and bruises being relatively minor, was back in her room; Father Steve was taking a shower, and the rest of the household was slowly getting back to their rooms. The Monseigneur was anxious to get back to his own bed, for he knew that tomorrow would be bringing a myriad of problems for him to deal with, one of which he was now certain, involved the loss of a truly cherished parish priest.

Chapter Twenty-three

Missy stood under the shower a long time trying to get the mental impressions she'd had of Frank's touch off of her skin. She had been very lucky and praised God for her timely rescue. And she thanked God for Father Steve. She didn't exactly know what was going to happen between the two of them, but he'd said he wanted her to come see him after she'd showered, and if he wanted her in his bedroom at four in the morning while the rest of the household slept, she tingled with excitement at what that meant. He had said he wanted to dispense with her chastity. Had he been joking, or had he actually meant it? And would she let him if he did? After all, she was a Catholic, and he was talking about premarital sex. She smiled. There was no doubt what she'd do. She'd revel in his touch. She'd give reverence to his body. She'd let him do any damn thing he wanted.

After toweling off, she picked up her torn and bloody nightgown, put it in the trash, and donned her old robe. Then she quietly made her way to Steve's room, tapped softly and opened the door. She stepped inside and closed the door noiselessly behind her.

"Lock it," Steve said. He was lying on the bed, one arm resting down by his side, the other under his head, propping it high on the pillow. He was covered with a sheet just to his hips, his bare masculine chest rising and falling slowly with each breath.

She locked the door and went to his bed. His gaze followed her, and in a clipped voice he said, "Lose the robe."

She untied the sash, shrugged her shoulders and let it fall to the floor. It glided down her body, pooling at her feet. He drank in every inch of her and slowly lifted the sheet. "Get In."

She moved to the side of the bed and slid in beside him. His skin felt cool against her fiery warmth. She longed to just lay beside him and absorb it.

When he turned and gathered her into his arms she could feel his bristly chest hairs rubbing against the tips of her nipples. He rolled over almost on top of her and propped himself over her with his elbows. His fingers caressed a damp curl by her ear, "You don't know how much I've missed you." His lips took hers in a kiss so sweet she wanted to sob from the sheer joy of it. He kissed her over and over, tasting and teasing. When his lips moved to her neck, he gave her languorous kisses all around her ear and murmured, "I'm going to take your virginity and make you mine now. Do you have any objections?" Soft lips continued their downward descent, his tongue stopping to lick lightly in the hollow at the base of her throat.

"No, it's been a damned nuisance, to be honest with you."

She felt his smile on the crest of her breast, and when his lips latched onto her nipple she thought she would soar to the moon. "Ahhh . . . " she sighed.

"Keep making noises like that, and I'm not sure how long I'll be able to hold off."

He moved his hand over her belly, his fingertips lightly grazing her as he found her tight curls, "I'm in a bit of a hurry this time, but next time, I want to savor you here with my tongue." He spread her thighs with his hand, and his fingertips found her sleek wet channel. Gently he pulled on one of her labial lips, then he gave it a quick, hard pinch. When her eyes darted to meet his, he whispered, "Just saving my place for later." His finger entered her. She welcomed him into her body. Another joined it and they moved inside her, touching all her secret places while she squirmed against him. Her inner core—the channel to her femininity—was begging for something more, something more substantial.

She needed to be filled, overwhelmed, and engorged—sated to full capacity. It was a feeling she'd never had before; she felt a void she hadn't even known existed in her body, as if she was an empty, hollow vessel yearning to be crammed to the top with steely, throbbing flesh. She was burning with the desire to have him enter her and satisfy her—to stretch her and possess her.

"I think you're ready," he said. "*Are* you ready?"

"I've been ready," she moaned.

He chuckled and positioned himself over her. She felt the velvety soft tip of his penis slide up and down between her lips. Then he shifted the upper part of his body away from her slightly and, using his thumb, he pushed his penis into place at her opening.

"Don't we need a condom?" she asked timidly.

"I've finally realized that God made you especially for me. He gave you to me, and He wants me to have you. I obviously want that very much, too," he said, his erection throbbing against her. "In giving you to me, he probably didn't have a condom in mind though. And being a very good Catholic boy, we won't worry about birth control. Is that all right with you?"

She simply nodded. He bent low to kiss her and thrust himself into her. He felt her maidenhead push back against him slightly, and using his hips he drove the full length of his member into her. He felt her stretch to house him and groaned with pleasure at her tightness as he was fully sheathed. Oh, what a heady feeling he thought as her hot channel completely encompassed him. He looked down into her face to gauge her reaction. She smiled up at him, and even though he could see the wetness of tears in her eyes, he knew she was all right with their coupling.

"I love you, Missy," he breathed as he retreated and then plunged into her. "I love you!" They worked themselves into a nice rhythm, each savoring the incredible feelings they were generating between them. Then, just when she thought things couldn't get any better, he sped up and plunged even deeper, a hard ridge of him pressing into an ultra-sensitive place on her. Suddenly, she gasped as she felt her body drop and spiral away, turning everything topsy-turvy as a wonderful explosion occurred deep inside her. On the fringes of her mind, she heard his groan then felt him pull out slightly before slamming forcefully back into her and seating himself deeply inside her before his hot jetting fluid spewed into her maiden cavity. He whimpered, his face contorted, and his mouth grimaced. Then his head fell beside hers on the pillow. It was as if he'd suddenly collapsed. She wondered if she'd done something wrong.

"Are you okay, Father Steve?" she whispered.

"Arrgghh," he moaned.

There was silence for a few moments, then he said. "You don't have to call me Father Steve anymore."

"What do I call you then?"

"Sweetheart, darling, husband, lover, or just plain ol' Steve works fine for me."

"Husband?"

"Husband."

"You'll never be Father Steve, again?"

"Honey, God frowns on his priests doing this," he said giving her a thrust of his hips, reminding her of his placement in her body. "I'll never be Father Steve again. Maybe a father who's name *is* Steve, if God blesses us from our many, many, unions." He moved his head so he could see her lips, then lowered his mouth, molding his lips to hers, and delighting in the sweet taste of her.

When he finished kissing her, he looked into her eyes. "You're not upset that I made love to you before I married you are you?"

"No. I didn't even know you wanted to marry me," she teased.

"I asked the Monseigneur to do it tonight, but he said it could wait 'til morning. But I couldn't."

She smiled up at him and said, "You're taking a lot for granted aren't you?"

He smiled down at her, "I've never proposed before, but I believe it's probably better to do it before you take the woman into your bed, terrify her with the sex act, and cause her great discomfort. Fortunately, I think you rather enjoyed your consummation, so I think I already know your answer." He reached for the nightstand where he had placed the little box he'd brought back from Europe. Using one hand, he flipped it open and faced the inside of it toward her. "Missy, will you marry me?"

Missy looked up to see a stunning 16th century, medieval-styled ring set with sapphires and diamonds in a delicate, silver filigreed setting. "Ohhh. It's lovely. Is it for me?"

"Do you see anybody else lying under me?" he asked with a chuckle, and watched while she took it out of box and put it on her finger.

"And your answer is?" he prompted.

"Oh, yes, yes. If I get to keep the ring, yes!"

He nuzzled her neck and laughed, "I was hoping you'd prefer to keep the man slightly more than the ring, but I'll settle for what I can get."

Then he felt her hips push up against him, "What do I get if we do it again?" she teased.

He hardened instantly, "Something that will remind you of fireworks and red-hot lava exploding in the sky," he said and pushed back against her.

"Show me."

"Gladly," he said as his lips took hers in a lusty kiss.

Chapter Twenty-four

Although Father Steve was pretty sure the Monseigneur knew what was going on in the bedroom of his errant priest, he knew that if he was flagrant enough to be caught with Missy in his bed, the Monseigneur's wrath would be severe. After all, this was a rectory and he was still technically a priest. So, before the sun came up, he walked Missy back to her old room, tucked her into the small bed and kissed her good night. They would be married at least in the eyes of God, if not in the eyes of the State, in the morning, and as soon as he could find a place for them to live, they would share the same bed again.

He knew he couldn't just leave the priesthood, that he had to be given permission to start a new life on the outside, and that there would be many people he'd have to talk to. But remembering the Monseigneur singing his "Climb every mountain" song, he knew he had a champion in his court and that it would all just be a simple matter of paperwork.

He had the inheritance from his mother to get them set up and to provide a supplemental income. He did have a doctorate, and he could still be a professor at the university, and that would enable Missy to continue her studies tuition-free. And best of all, he had the love of a wonderful God who had given him Missy. Everything was going to be just fine.

He would find them a nice little house near the college so he could teach and she could study. During the summers he'd take her to Europe and show her all the beautiful cities. And they'd have babies, lots of babies, new little Catholics that the Monseigneur would christen for him. He'd still be active in the church— probably teach several Catechism classes, maybe even mow the lawn on cool summer evenings. But he wouldn't call Bingo, and he wouldn't sit next to Mrs. Reynolds at Pot Luck Dinners, and he wouldn't hear a single confession, ever, ever again.

He went back to his room and picked up the little stuffed elephant from his dresser. Yes, everything would be just fine. The only thing left was the elephant that Missy had said was between them.

Frank . . . the elephant, the source of so much anguish was a major problem for him. He'd divulged a confidence that he wasn't supposed to. He was responsible for where Frank was now, in the hospital under detention, soon to be charged with rape, murder, kidnapping and attempted rape. He didn't feel sorry for Frank, not in the slightest. But he did feel that he had let down the priesthood as a whole. It was bad enough that he'd broken his vow of celibacy, but that hadn't hurt anyone, and he was happy it was the reason he was giving up the priesthood as his career, but he'd betrayed a solemn, scared trust. What happened in the confessional was inviolate. No manner of coercion— State, Federal or Ecclesiastical could force a priest to relay what was in a sinner's heart. Yet, he'd done it, just the same. Well, he hadn't actually done it yet.

He hadn't laid the blame or pointed the finger, but he had used the knowledge. And now all the connections would be made. He would leave the priesthood in shame and disgrace. They would whisper about him for years: "There's the ex-priest who can't keep his mouth shut; there's the defrocked celebrant who can't keep a secret; you don't want him to be a prisoner with you; he doesn't even require torture to blab all he knows." It wouldn't matter that the crime had involved his own family, no one would see the irony in that, they would just see the dishonor in him. He tossed the elephant onto the bed and went into his bathroom to shower and dress for the day.

Before leaving his room, he sat at his desk, thought long and hard, and then with all the integrity he could muster, he wrote a factual encapsulation of his betrayal of Frank's sacred confession to him. He tucked the letter into an envelope, addressed it to the Monseigneur, and sealed it. He left it in the center of the desk in the Monseigneur's bedroom study.

When he went downstairs, he was surprised to see Missy sitting in the parlor with the Monseigneur and two police officers. They informed him that Frank was still in critical care, but that he was expected to recover and would then be transferred to the county jail to await charges. Missy had already told them that Father Steve had been the one to discover Frank in the act of committing rape, and that he had been the one who had detained him and safeguarded her.

"Detained?" one of the officers scoffed. "He looks like he was dragged behind a truck!"

"He was very angry to be interrupted," Missy said.

"Missy . . . " Father Steve said, admonishing her

to tell the truth.

"He was!" she defended. "He was obsessed with taking my virginity. He even told me his first virgin was stolen from him and that he killed her and her mother. Her name was Kelly. That was your sister's name, wasn't it Father Steve?" Frank hadn't told her the girl's name, but she knew it was Kelly, she knew it was Father Steve's sister, even Frank knew now that it had been Father Steve's sister and mother that he'd killed. He knew she was giving him the chance to let it all come out without anyone knowing about the confession. "Could he have been the one who killed your sister and mother?" she asked, trying to tie it up for everyone, in case someone hadn't already made the connection.

She looked at the officers who had both stopped writing. "He confessed to me that he raped and killed a girl and her mother. He told me once he raped me, I would adore him, that from then on I would be his for all eternity. He seemed to really believe this. He was convinced that I somehow belonged to him. If Father Steve hadn't found us when he did, I would have been raped. He was determined to make me his. Father Steve had no choice but to physically restrain him."

"Physically restrain him? Miss Roberts, this man has a jaw broken in two places, a fractured eye socket, multiple contusions, a ruptured spleen, a concussion and there's practically nothing left of his nose."

"Well in light of what I just told you about Father Steve's sister and mother, are you going to hold that against him?"

"Did he know this?"

"I'm sure when he saw all that was happening, it could have easily triggered his memory of his sister and caused him to take some of his emotions out on the man who was trying to rape me. Let's remember who the victim is here!" she said sharply.

"Did you go to the clinic?"

"I wasn't actually raped. He was just about to . . . " she shivered and started softly sobbing, then she continued, "He was just about to when Father Steve pulled him off of me."

Just then another officer came into the room. Father Steve recognized him as Detective Samuels, one of the officers who had worked on his sister's case, the one he had spoken to on the phone several weeks ago.

"We got him, Father Steve. We finally found that missing semen sample. It matches the DNA we took from him a few weeks ago. He's definitely the man who killed your mother and your sister."

Both officers flipped their notebooks closed. "Well, Father, it doesn't appear that you used excessive force after all. Too bad you didn't have a baseball bat handy for his knees."

Father Steve slumped down into the nearest chair. It was over. It was finally over. He looked at Missy and she smiled at him. He winked back, "Okay, I guess I punished him enough for what he tried to do to Missy. Now what are *you* guys going to do to punish him for what he did to my mother and sister? What do we have to do to keep him from trying to do this again? How much time is he likely to get for the murders?"

"Let's just say you don't have to worry about him getting close to any virgins again unless they hire one as a prison guard. Which, judging from the ones I've met, is not very likely to happen."

The Monseigneur married Steve and Missy privately that afternoon, having been unsuccessful in his attempts to urge Steve to wait the four weeks that were customary to allow for the Banns to be announced in the parish newsletter. But Father Steve had been adamant, he knew they couldn't be legally married; it would take a few days to secure a license, when the Monseigneur would marry them again with witnesses—but he wanted to be married in the eyes of God as soon as possible.

After the brief ceremony in the church, and while everyone was enjoying the hastily prepared reception buffet, the Monseigneur took Father Steve aside and scolded him. "Never put that kind of stuff in writing, never, never, never. It's all pointless anyway—the outcome wouldn't have changed for Frank. Even if you'd kept every scrap a secret, not responded to the knowledge that you had, he would have been discovered. The only exception was, this time, his victim was spared," he said indicating a laughing Missy, being hugged by her friends. "Apparently, it was God's will that you know Frank's identity and have the capability to protect Missy. So now, you can further do his bidding by becoming her husband. And, of course, the father of many, many Catholic babies," he said with a big grin. He waved his wrinkled hand in the air as if signifying the banality of all the rules, tenets, and procedures they always had to adhere to, "I burned it. No one but He needs to know," he said pointing toward the ceiling and beyond, "and I believe he orchestrates everything for a reason. Go kiss your bride."

It was announced at the next mass that Father Steve was leaving the priesthood. The entire congregation was stunned. Everyone that is, except

Mrs. Reynolds, who decided it was time to switch to a new parish, maybe even a new diocese. She had enjoyed the Mass when Father Steve had celebrated it, when she could fantasize about what might happen between them. There was no way she would be able to be in the same church with him and his new bride as they held hands and smiled at each other.

Missy's father and stepmother showed up in time for the legal wedding ceremony. Friends of Steve's put the message out on all the Internet camping blogs and word traveled from camper to camper until it reached their ears in San Antonio. They pulled up in their Holiday Rambler the morning of the wedding and her father walked her down the aisle. He promised to do a better job of staying in touch when he kissed her on the cheek just before handing her over to the groom.

The first night of their honeymoon was spent in their new bungalow among cluttered boxes and wedding presents. The only piece of furniture so far, was the big king-sized bed Steve had purchased and arranged to have delivered the day before.

Missy came out of the master bathroom in a new nightgown, one of several she had received as gifts from her husband. Steve was waiting for her in bed, his back propped against the headboard, his hands behind his head.

"There's one thing I need to know," she said.

"What's that sweetheart?"

"What in the world is my new last name? I vaguely remember the Monseigneur saying your whole name, but I'm not sure I heard it right."

He laughed and leaped out of the bed, gathered her up in his arms and spun with her around the room. "You are now Mrs. Stephen Ignatius Tyndale."

"Ignatius?"

"I may be named after the saints but let me tell you, there isn't going to be anything saintly going on in this room tonight." He carried her to the bed and laid her gently against the pillows.

She noticed the little stuffed elephant that was at the foot of the bed. "Why did you bring that in here?"

"I plan on propping your sweet little bottom up in the air with it. That way you'll know for certain, that it's no longer *between* us."

"Mmmm, next thing I know you'll be at one of those sex shops getting a harness."

He flinched and moved back from her, shocked. "Where in the world did you ever hear about one of those?"

"I told you . . . I read a lot."

He nuzzled her neck and murmured, "I think I'm going to have to censure your reading material from now on."

"Why?" she said as she grinned and saucily pulled down a strap of her nightgown, baring one small, perfectly rounded breast.

"Mmmm," he said, taking the hard little peak into his mouth. "I've been celibate for a long, long time. I think I'm going to be content with the missionary position for quite some time."

"Bet me," she said as she bucked her hips, rolled him onto his back and straddled him.

He lifted her nightgown over her head and tossed it aside, then gingerly impaled her with his throbbing erection, letting her body adjust to each incremental inch of his erection before feeding her another. "On second thought, I have always been a firm believer in the First Amendment."

"Good, because I just started reading the Kama Sutra."

"Ohhhh," he groaned, and she wasn't sure it was because of what she'd said, or what she just did with her hips. But he looked happy—so she did it again, and again. And again.

The End

About the Author

Jacqueline DeGroot has published ten novels, a book of short stories and co-authored a local history book. She is active in several writing groups and helps new writers get their manuscripts published.

Jack lives in Sunset Beach with her husband Bill. Daughter Kimberly recently graduated from UNCW, and two grown sons live in Shallotte and New York. Formerly an overachieving car salesperson in Vienna, VA—she ranked #6 in the country in Pontiac sales—Jack now enjoys full moon parties at the beach, a nice bottle of LaTerre and camping trips with Bill in their "new" motorhome.

www.ingramcontent.com/pod-product-compliance
Lightning Source LLC
Chambersburg PA
CBHW060112260626
47160CB00005B/1871